Captured

ISBN: 978-1-9991282-3-4

Irae

Kira saw the smoke wafting above the city of Irae and smiled. There were no humans to be found here during the Scorch, an annual event marked by fires intended to drive out pests, but still she sensed a presence amidst the recently abandoned structures. Her hair flailed against the crimson sky, the tousled strands as black as burnt wood as she removed the bag of supplies and set it on the ground.

"Well, we're above the problem," came a voice from behind her. "I'm not seeing a solution though."

"Maybe we're not high enough," she suggested as her partner, Mason, appeared at her side. Like her, he wore a heat-resistant bodysuit, boots, and carried a trove of tools on his back, their uses ranging from basic repairs to more complicated applications—like trapping demons, for instance. Neither the weight of his burden nor the purpose of their mission seemed to cause him much angst. "Maybe we'll have better luck once we reach the mountains," Kira added.

"I wouldn't count on it. If the wind changes direction, it'll turn the mountainside into a giant oven. I vote we stick to the forest."

"And risk losing the malevolent's trail? I don't think so."

Kira rummaged through the pack until she uncovered a small, rectangular device. Kneeling down, she cleared a circle in the carpet of leaves and set the device in the soil, where four metallic legs unfolded from the edges of the contraption and rooted themselves into the ground. The screen hummed to life, and soon a miniature projection of Irae and the surrounding landscape sprang up to greet them.

"We're here," she said, zooming in on their location. Mason squinted at the hologram, watching the miniature projection of himself mirror his every move. "The malevolent is here, in the mountains. By my estimation, we have less than thirty minutes to track, trap, and transport it back to the Commander. To save time, I suggest we cut through the valley."

Kira picked up the scanner, causing the legs to retract as the screen went dark. She tossed it into the bag and hoisted it onto her shoulders before turning to her partner.

"I know Ansel isn't a fan of shortcuts, but it's the only chance we have of completing the mission." She began walking, and Mason fell into step beside her.

"You know what else he isn't a fan of?" he asked as they picked their way over the stumps and branches. "Burning to a crisp on the side of a mountain."

"There are worse ways to die." Not that Kira had any experience with death—or living. Her mother had died slowly of cancer, suffering through her final months of life as a human before passing into a new one as a Spirit Catcher. She was an expert at dying and dealing with the dead, at guiding them through their trauma and inevitable rebirth, but when it came to kindling a relationship with her daughter, she had nothing on the citizens of Irae.

Kira and Mason traveled at a spirited pace among the flowering trees and tall grasses. Earlier that day, the fields cushioning the city had been a shimmering sea of violet; now, they were a deep emerald, with patches of chartreuse cropping up here and there. A winged creature with black tail feathers and long, cat-like limbs scampered up a nearby tree, vanishing into the profusion of papery white petals.

"In a few hours, all of this will be ash," Mason remarked, offering Kira the flower he'd plucked off a low-hanging branch. She buried her nose in its sweet scent, momentarily forgetting about the smoke and her mother. "Makes you appreciate how fragile life is."

"I wouldn't know."

Mason nudged her shoulder and smiled. "Then you're one of the lucky ones."

Once they'd reached the mountain pass, they stopped again and Kira removed her bag to retrieve a rosewood box.

"Who's building the orb?" Mason asked as she tucked the vessel under her arm and hooked her hand through the strap once again.

"I am," she replied. "Do you have the scout?"

Mason lowered himself to the ground, removed his pack, and pulled out a sleek, softball-sized gadget. Shortly after he'd come to The Establishment, he received a specialized ring called a Keepsake, which not only preserved his memories from his past life, but also changed colour in the presence of malevolents. However, it was impossible to see what colour the stone was under his glove, so the scout would have to do the job for him.

He opened his hand. The scout sprouted eight legs and panned its lens over the jagged terrain, its infrared sensor combing the cracks and crevices for heat. Hot on the malevolent's trail, it scurried off Mason's palm before disappearing between two rocks, its metallic feet clicking industriously on the argillite slabs.

Kira placed the box on the ground and undid the clasp. Ansel had gifted the vessel to her on the assumption that its unusual history would bring her luck, but so far all it had done was add unnecessary weight to an already heavy bag.

Mason glanced up at the sky. Long, fiery coils of heat curled through the clouds of dust and debris. Kira tipped back the lid on the wooden box and scanned the mountainside for the arachnoid gadget, her anxiety mounting when it failed to return.

That's when she heard it: the high, piercing cry of a malevolent being driven out of its lair like a frightened rabbit from its burrow. Like most demonic entities, it had seething red eyes, an abundance of teeth, and a hunched, emaciated frame covered in coarse hair like a wolf's. Judging by its size, Kira estimated it to be three hundred years old—barely an infant, at least by the afterlife's standards. And babies were always hungry.

Kira brought her hands together, leaving less than an inch of space between her fingers. Blue light pulsed against her gloved palms as she summoned her most vivid memories from the depths of her Keepsake. The clearer the vision, the more powerful the orb. Not that she had much to draw on, having been raised in The Establishment—a place where the dead were given a chance to earn another shot at life. The malevolent snarled like an ornery dog, until, at last, Kira clapped her hands and distributed the energy.

The monster extended to its full height and batted its claws at the thickening air and blinding light. These were creatures of darkness: they dwelled in the shadows of society, feasted on fear and desperation, and made Hell look like a fairytale. They were also surprisingly easy to control, at least at this age. Kira indicated the antique box at her feet, and the malevolent surrendered with a squeal, seeking the safety of the vessel over the heat of the mountain that was rapidly turning to rubble.

As boulders toppled down around them, the scout rolled across the shifting ground and into Mason's hand. Kira snapped a lock on the vessel, stuffed it into her bag, and was racing after him before she could even congratulate herself on another successful quarantine.

They sprinted across the hodgepodge town, where a flurry of flaming petals filled the smoky grey air. The trees ignited in a wave of amber, sending the last of the winged creatures fleeing for the more densely foliaged woodland to the south. Kira glanced back at the burning town as the cluster of homes and businesses was reduced to ashes.

They charged up the hill and into the forest, where the canopies of the trees were decorated in glowing red embers. Mason bobbed along the trail a few feet ahead, glancing back occasionally to assure himself of Kira's presence before hanging a left and disappearing between two bushes.

Through the wall of hot, bitter smoke, the outline of a spacecraft emerged. The Commander 2 sat in the middle of a clearing, dwarfed by the trees towering overhead. As soon as they'd crested the last knoll leading from the forest, a hatch opened and a ladder appeared. Mason ushered Kira up the metal rungs as the carpet of leaves combusted under their feet, throwing heat into the circular opening.

Having reached the top of the ladder, Kira scuttled sideways, leaving barely enough room for Mason to scramble into the decontamination bay before the hatch clanged shut behind them.

He rolled onto his back and instinctively laid a hand on his chest, noting grimly the absence of movement. He was nothing more than energy now: a smudge of movement in the corner of a room, a memory that got fainter with each passing year, a ghost with nowhere and nothing to haunt. All Catchers were surrounded by an invisible membrane—humans sometimes called it an aura—that helped them process changes in their environment, and right now, his felt itchier than a wool sweater. He shifted slightly to relieve the discomfort in his shoulders and turned to look at Kira.

"And you wanted to stick to the woods," Kira reminded him with a smirk. She dragged her bag onto her lap and pulled out the box, which she set on the floor between them.

He smiled. "Next time, perhaps we should plan better and not procrastinate. Or do you just love the thrill of doing everything last minute?"

She shrugged. "When you don't fear death, you don't fear time."

"I guess that attitude makes sense, knowing who your mother is."

Picking up the container, Kira stepped over him and walked to the door. "I've been told I get my attitude from my father."

"Ah. The infamous Gabe Conway." Mason stood up and followed her through the opening. "He'd be so proud."

"My father was a proud man in all the wrong ways. Don't put him on a pedestal."

Walking to the centre of the room, Kira placed the vessel on a stand and approached a nearby screen to log their latest addition. Behind her, Mason began to remove the bodysuit, beginning with the transparent facemask and working his way down to his boots.

"No pedestals here," he remarked as she continued to input the data, "just plain, old-fashioned observation. You may be an exceptional case, but at least you inherited all the right qualities: courage, integrity, and enough attitude to get the job done right the first time."

Despite herself, Kira smiled. "If I didn't know better, I'd think you were trying to flatter me."

She put the finishing touches on her report and turned toward the stand. The floor beneath the pedestal twisted open and they watched as the rosewood box was lowered into the holding tank.

"That's another one down," Mason said as the floor sealed itself and Kira removed her bodysuit to reveal the red uniform underneath. "So, what are you planning to do when we finally go home?"

"I haven't thought about it—mainly because I don't want to."

The lines around Mason's mouth softened. "It's been five years, Kira. You must be feeling at least a little homesick by now."

Balling up the bodysuit, Kira opened the hatch to the Commander's laundry hamper and stuffed the garment inside. The Establishment was the only home she'd ever known, but it got lonely: nobody stuck around for long once they realized they could earn their freedom. Even Mason would be gone one day, and he understood her better than her mother ever could. When that happened, then maybe Kira would finally understand what it meant to be homesick.

"I try not to get too attached," she explained, shutting the hatch. "The stars are my home, and the planets and the moons and even that patch of space debris you said looked like—like a—"

"Like sprinkles on a cupcake," he finished, chuckling. "You remember that?"

Kira held up her left hand to show off the Keepsake. "How could I forget? Though I'm still confused about what a cupcake is, or why humans seem to love them so much."

"Next life," he promised, cupping his hands over her shoulders. "I'll teach you everything you need to know."

A sinking feeling filled the hollow space under Kira's ribs. Breaking out of Mason's hold, she continued toward the secondary decontamination bay, where the remaining pathogens were cleansed from her uniform by means of ultraviolet light. She exited the bay so Mason could undergo the same process, then fell into step with him as they made their way back to the cockpit.

"Something tells me there won't be a next life," Kira said as they climbed a flight of stairs to a circular room featuring six seats clustered under a glass dome. The rest of the crew barely looked up from their instrument panels as the pair appeared. "My quotas are basically infinite."

"That's only because you're so talented. If they capped you at a million souls, you'd be out of here in six months." Mason slid into one of the vacant chairs and slipped on his headset.

Across the aisle, Kira settled into her own workstation and faced a screen so he wouldn't notice her smiling. "Stop flattering me, Mr. Massey."

"Massey," came a voice from the front of the Commander, "we're airborne. Where to next?"

Mason consulted his multitude of screens, pausing to appraise one in detail as he directed his words back at the source of the inquiry.

"Aroya," he announced, minimizing the radar and pulling up another, "home to a cesspool of malicious spirits with a hankering for mutant fauna. Oh, how I love nuclear wastelands."

"How many malevolents are we escorting?" Kira asked as the burning city of Irae was reduced to a pinprick of light.

"Sixty-four."

"Sounds like the malevolent population on Aroya is thriving."

"Hardly surprising. They've had fifty-two thousand years to adapt." Mason grinned at Kira and double-checked his restraint. "Ready when you are, Dean."

Dean reached for the lever on the controls, and the fireball vanished from sight.

The Dying Light

"There it is," a voice echoed in the glass bubble. "Home sweet home."

The Commander buzzed with anticipation as the familiar outline of a hangar came into view, its open bay gaping like a frog's mouth. Kira had been dreading this moment since they'd collected their last specimen, but didn't want to sink her teammates' spirits with an audible groan of displeasure.

"Headquarters, this is Commander 2," Casey Carlisle, who was piloting the spacecraft, said into the headset. "Docking bay is in sight. Seeking permission to dock."

The void crackled to life in her ear. "Permission to dock granted, Commander 2."

Casey covered the microphone and looked over at Dean. "Any last words before Ansel destroys you?"

"I regret nothing." Dean set his jaw and stared down his fate as if it was a grizzly, displaying no fear in his final moments.

Casey angled the microphone back toward her mouth. "Headquarters, this is Casey Carlisle. I've initiated the docking process and will require ground support in approximately fifteen seconds."

"Acknowledged, Miss Carlisle. Ground support dispatched."

Mason leaned on the armrest. "Hey. It's going to be okay. I promise."

"What's the number one rule in the afterlife?" Kira shifted her gaze from the gap between Casey and Dean's seats. "No promises."

"I'm making an exception for you." Turning back to the controls, Mason closed his eyes and ignored the apprehension tingling in his spine. As much as he wanted to ascribe Dean's actions to fear, his treatment of the infected human on Aroya lacked the momentary pause given to compassion for another life. And Kira, who'd been infected in the womb, was no safer around Dean than she was amidst the inferno of Irae.

Casey concentrated on the multitude of gages as each stable instrument pinged approvingly, confirming the Commander's vertical and horizontal alignment as well as its final approach speed. She soon took her hands off the controls, allowing the spacecraft to ease itself into position as an army of support personnel swarmed the platform. Kira glanced around at the pristine facilities and spotted Ansel's head, smooth as carved marble, amongst the helmeted horde. He didn't seem angry or tense, though most days it was difficult to tell if he felt anything at all. Mason, on the other hand, would've made a very realistic statue.

"Nervous?" Kira asked, tearing her mind away from Ansel's stoicism as she faced her partner.

"What makes you say that?"

"I can feel your energy from here."

"I'm not nervous," he said as shadows engulfed the cockpit. "Just because there's a chance I may not survive to see another mission is no reason for a few butterflies in my stomach."

Kira furrowed her brows. "What?"

"It's an expression. Like the heebie-jeebies."

She removed the headset, but her features remained scrunched and twisted in the glow of the dashboard. "Humans are so strange."

"You have no idea." And she didn't, really. Humans *were* strange, but in ways even members of their own kind failed to comprehend. The Establishment had rules, protocols, and straight lines; humanity had emotions (which often got mixed), exceptions, and the egregious notion of guarantees. Everything Kira knew about humans she'd learned from books, but even Ansel, who knew everything, couldn't explain some of the more peculiar aspects of mankind's existence—like why they fell in love when it wasn't necessary for the continuation of their specie, or why some kept injecting themselves with poison when all they wanted was to heal. Mason rubbed his arm, but the scars had vanished years ago—and with them, his knowledge of what it meant to be human. To live.

Lifting the shoulder bars over his head, Mason rose and stepped out from behind the controls. Kira flipped the master switch on her instrument panel, dimming the indicators and screens spread across the console, then followed him to the exit, where they descended the metal ramp to join the rest of the crew on the floor.

"Ah, Kira," Ansel said as she appeared, "just the individual I wanted to see."

Kira stiffened. Beside her, Mason lowered his voice and said, "Don't assume anything. Just hear him out."

Confusion stirred in Ansel's wizened expression. "Is there a problem, Mr. Massey?"

"No, sir."

Turning his focus back to Kira, Ansel gave a discreet nod and said, "Perhaps Kira and I should continue this conversation in my office…"

"On second thought," Mason amended, "you'd better assume the worst."

"And I'll be seeing you afterwards, Mr. Massey." Addressing the others, Ansel said, "The rest of you may go. Should you have any concerns, I urge you to take them up with your mentors."

The crew disbanded, leaving Kira and Mason standing in the middle of the hangar while a flurry of technicians attended to the Commander.

"If this is about what happened on Aroya," Kira preempted, earning a bewildered look from Mason and a slightly less startled one from Ansel, "I just want you to know that we had no intention of sabotaging the mission. Dean was concerned about the crew's safety and didn't want the situation to escalate."

Ansel's gaze settled on hers. As always, his expression held less emotion than the tiles on the floor, each one polished to a blistering shine that made the sun look lacklustre by comparison.

"I'm sure Mr. Weiss's intentions were nothing short of heroic. However, after carefully reviewing your case, I'm afraid there are some things we need to discuss. Kira, if you'll come with me…"

Ansel motioned for her to follow. Were these the butterflies Mason had been referring to earlier? Kira wondered as she was overcome with an urge to take flight. Maybe she could convince Mason to join her; he knew how to pilot the Commander 2 as well as she did. After all, if there was anyone who *didn't* deserve to be punished, it was him.

Mason turned to the woman on his right. She hadn't moved an inch from where she stood, but one look into her eyes told him her mind was a million miles away.

"Kira," he began, "I—"

"I told you not to make any promises," she intoned, taking up a brisk pace. She climbed the stairs to the observation deck and vanished through the doors.

If he were still human, Mason reflected, this would be the part where he released a breath; he would have to settle for staring after her instead. Perhaps the strangest part of humanity was the inherent cruelty of its greatest weapon: hope.

●

"This is so unfair! Can't you talk to him?"

"What's unfair about it? You were out of line. If you ask me, Ansel's decision to demote you was more than fair."

Sarah leaned back in her chair and studied the stack of books awaiting her input on the desk. In light of Kira's transgression, she'd been forced to let her usual commitments fall by the wayside. This was how The Establishment handled all mishaps: first, the employee in question was required to submit an incident report citing the offense in its entirety, including the date, time, location, and any resulting human casualties, if applicable. From there, the incident report was forwarded to his or her immediate supervisor, who would review the case, determine the magnitude of the error, and propose an appropriate course of action.

This feedback was then directed to Ansel, who either approved the punishment or requested additional insight, before approaching the offending employee to deliver the verdict. But this time was different. This time, it wasn't just a professional decision Sarah was making, but a personal one, too.

"And you can't always expect me to bail you out," Sarah said firmly. "I realize you're an exceptional case, but that doesn't absolve you of responsibility."

"But why demote me? Why not just send me to the basement? Mason got to go to the basement."

"Mason didn't kill a human citizen."

"He would've died anyway. What was I supposed to do?"

"Exactly what you were trained to do: isolate and purify. That's how we handle organic possessions."

Kira began to pace, sending ripples of annoyance through Sarah's field.

"You don't get it," Kira started, doubling back on her tracks, "you don't know what it's like to be me. You don't understand the pressure."

"You think I don't understand pressure? How do you think I got this job—by wishing on a star?"

"That's another thing," Kira spat, "you're so—so—"

"Kira, centre yourself. I can feel your energy from here."

"—So high and mighty all the time! Just because you saved humanity from extinction doesn't make you a hero, you know."

"Kira, sit down."

"Oh, make me, mother."

Sarah directed her attention at the corner of the room and twitched her fingers, beckoning the ornately carved bergère chair. The hotheaded young Catcher landed in the padded seat with a grunt. Kira strained against the artificial gravity, her lucid green eyes blazing with rage.

"When you're ready to discuss this situation like an adult, I'll give you back your energy," Sarah explained calmly.

Kira lunged, only to be sucked back into the chair's beastly presence.

"You know that incident report was only half the story," she began as Sarah returned to her work. "Dean should be punished, too. After all, it was his idea to seek and destroy."

Sarah tore her eyes from the screen and fixed her daughter with a grimace.

"So you're telling me," Sarah said slowly, "that in addition to making an unauthorized claim, you also filed an incomplete incident report?"

Kira clamped her mouth shut. When Mason was upset, he used strange words to express himself, but none of them came to her now.

"Kira," Sarah persisted, "answer me."

Kira shut her eyes. Memories flashed across the black canvas: images of Aroya in all its radioactive glory. In her mind, she saw a wounded human hobbling for the safety of his concrete bunker. He had managed to escape the malevolents once, but with the infection burning through his bloodstream, he was unlikely to survive the night. Mason had believed he could be saved, but Dean was in charge—and like the shadowy hunters prowling Aroya's underbrush, he lived for the kill.

Infiltrating the human's shelter had been a simple matter of hacking the security system. Once inside, they'd discovered a trail of blood, dark red and bubbling like lava, leading to a windowless room. A gas mask had been discarded in the doorway, and the foul sweetness of gangrene hung in the air above a soiled mattress.

Kira had knelt beside the bed and taken the man's hand. There'd been no fear in his eyes, only a desperate yearning for relief from his pain.

"It's okay," she'd whispered, "we're here to help." The human had smiled. That was a good sign, according to Ansel.

"He's beyond help," Dean had stated. "We need to destroy him."

"Dean—"

Dean had raised his hand, silencing Mason's protests. "I won't take the chance that he turns on us. Once the toxin spreads to his brain, he won't see us as allies anymore." He'd turned back to the victim, whose hands and face were covered in boils. "He'll see us as the enemy. As prey."

"It's against protocol," Mason had argued, stepping forward.

"It's us, or him. You choose."

Mason couldn't decide, so Dean had made the choice for them. He'd gathered his clearest memories into a neat blue orb, then flattened it against the human's chest—but not before Mason grabbed Kira's arm and wrenched her free from certain death. Had she still been clutching the man's hand when Dean delivered his fatal blow, his orb would have destroyed her, too.

Sarah's voice stripped the darkness from Kira's thoughts, bringing her back to the present. "That human citizen was the last of his kind. Do you know what this means?"

Her daughter nodded solemnly. "Extinction."

"And what happens when humans go extinct?"

"Anarchy." Kira shook her head. "Dean didn't think he stood a chance. He was already infected by the time we found him in his bunker."

"Which is why you carry neutralizers on every mission."

"He had open sores and a rash," Kira argued.

"That's only stage one! He had a ninety-five percent chance of survival." Sarah composed herself. "You never seek and destroy a human vessel. An object vessel, yes, but never a human."

"But you destroyed a human vessel years ago! Remember the lair?"

"That wasn't a human, Kira, that was a malevolent masquerading as a human. They know the laws and they know most Hunters will hesitate when they see a human form, thus granting them a point of entry. That's why you always engage before you proceed with quarantine." Sarah stood up. "Where's Dean?"

"In the decompression chamber, I'd assume." Kira faltered. "What are you going to do to him?"

"I'm not going to do anything. Rogue Catchers are Ansel's specialty." Sighing, Sarah pressed a button in the corner of the desk. "Celeste, could you come in here, please?"

The door slid open. Celeste folded her hands in front of her skirt, awaiting Sarah's orders.

"Celeste, please escort my daughter to the barracks."

"Of course. Will you require guards?"

Kira's eyes stumbled over to her mother, who drummed the desk while she thought.

"I don't think that will be necessary this time." With a gentle movement of her hand, she unpinned Kira from the chair.

The office door opened again, and Kira stormed out without another look back.

Hostile Encounters

Kira was shaking. Celeste had brought her to the barracks in hopes the quiet atmosphere and soft lighting would help calm her mind, but now that she was alone, Kira saw no reason for restraint. Dean had tried to destroy her—not just on Aroya, but on several other occasions in which he believed he could make it look like an accident. The worst part was that the rest of the crew looked up to him, since he'd been a game hunter in his previous life and considered himself overqualified for the job he currently held. Killing was in his blood, like malevolence was in hers.

Kira rested her elbows on her knees and studied her hands. A faint, blue glow washed over her unblemished skin and brought out the flecks of metal trapped in her ring. Every Keepsake was as unique as its wearer, but hers had been designed a little differently: the amalgamation of chromite and copper gave the ring unparalleled strength and heat resistance while enabling her to conduct electricity. *A powerful ring for a powerful spirit* was how Ansel had described it. Normally, powerful spirits—malevolents—were housed in the basement, a safe distance from the docile but largely defenseless Catcher population. Not Kira, though; she was the exception. Maybe Mason had been onto something when he called her one of the lucky ones.

The door opened. Sarah stood outside, talking to Celeste. When she saw Kira watching them, she dismissed her associate, then entered the room with an air of cautious sympathy.

"I remember my first time in the barracks," Sarah began. "Ansel was teaching me how to quarantine that day. The day I was… inoculated."

"You mean infected," Kira returned.

Sarah shook her head and sat down next to Kira.

"After I collapsed in the Ward, I thought I'd been infected," she explained. "Ansel had promised he would destroy me if that happened, but I woke up some time later in the infirmary. He told me that I'd used a corrupt image as the final link in my memory chain, and it gave the malevolent a false entry point. I have the ability to repel evil spirits so long as they don't have access to my essence."

Sarah pressed her fingers against her abdomen. A white light streamed from her pores, penetrating the blouse she wore and illuminating the hollow cavity of her human shell. Inside, a fist-sized orb lay cradled in the network of nerve endings. Every being possessed an essence—even humans, though most of them didn't realize it, or simply chose not to believe in the existence of a soul. But it was there, and unlike Kira's, it was blue.

"If you can repel evil spirits, why didn't you repel me?" Kira asked.

Sarah lowered her hand.

"I couldn't," she answered. "Once you'd established yourself, you fed on my energy until I was too weak to function."

A miniature version of Irae spread through Kira's cheeks. Catchers didn't blush, but malevolents were unfamiliar with the concept of shame. It was a strange sensation to be so disoriented in her own skin. "I'm sorry for feeding on you. Apparently, I was evil before I even knew what that word meant…"

"You weren't evil, and you still aren't. Disobedient at times, but that can be fixed." Getting to her feet, she faced her daughter. "Speaking of obedience, I spoke to Ansel."

Kira's ears perked. "And?"

"And he's agreed to reconsider your demotion." A flicker of hope kindled in Kira's eyes, which Sarah snuffed with a stern motion of her hand. "That being said, there are no guarantees. I've bought you a bit of time, but if you want your job back, you're going to have to work for it."

"But I already have!" Kira fumed. "I've completed all three levels of Quarantine, learned how to reverse a malevolent bite, and I can practically operate the Commander 2 blindfolded. What more can I possibly do?"

"Ansel wants to see that you understand the gravity of your actions. His punishment is meant to teach you patience."

"Patience," Kira scoffed. "And what's Dean learning—how to get away with murder?"

"Dean is being dealt with," Sarah said in a measured tone, "but you and Mason are equally responsible for what happened on Aroya.

The purpose of a team is to work together. That's why you'll be joining Mason in the basement, starting today."

"The basement?"

"You'll be spending the foreseeable future performing custodial duties: cleaning the tanks, doing repairs, and most importantly, *not* socializing with Mason. Depending on how well you follow orders, Ansel may even give you a reduced sentence." Sarah paused. "Do we have an agreement?"

"Yes."

"Good. I'll let Jonathon know you're on your way down."

●

"Welcome to the Jonathon Borg school of Demonic Species Management. Today's lesson will focus on habitat purification and temporary rehoming. I've identified a series of enclosures that will need to be purged and repaired prior to being sterilized and re-populated, but first, allow me to explain the malevolents' role in powering The Establishment."

"But we already know how they power The Establishment," Kira protested, a warm, pink hue expanding across her high-boned cheeks until it looked like she might burst with impatience.

"Hear him out," Mason muttered. "The sooner he finishes talking, the sooner he'll leave us alone."

Jonathon's mouth tightened at the corners. He'd been tasked with keeping Ansel's subjects out of trouble—and away from each other. They would both be alone soon enough, but not in the way Mason hoped.

"As I was saying," Jonathon continued. "You'll want to ensure there are no structural defects. The walls have been reinforced, but you know how persistent malevolents can be, so a certain amount of damage is inevitable."

He picked up the buckets of cleaning solution and handed one to each employee.

"Mason will start with the tanks on the south side. You will be responsible for everything west of the main generator," Jonathon said, maintaining his grip on the metal handle. He leaned forward, letting his next words wash over Kira like a river. "And if you try to leave, we'll skip ahead to lesson two: emergency containment and crisis mitigation."

"My mother didn't tell me you were so funny," Kira frosted, jerking the pail of solvent free from Jonathon's steely grip. The bubbles on the surface of the chemical concoction swirled into a scale model of the Milky Way, with her luminous reflection at the centre.

"Why spoil the surprise?" He waved a hand at the maze of glass and concrete stretching a hundred miles in each direction. Kira and Mason traded looks, then he turned and headed for the cluster of monstrous aquariums without another word.

The basement contained dozens of generators, the primary one being the approximate size and shape of a train car. Kira only knew what a train was because her mother had described this peculiar mode of transportation in the human realm: elongated pods joined end to end and propelled along metal tracks, with switches to guide them away from danger. Except sometimes the switches failed, and sometimes danger was unavoidable.

Kira climbed the ladder to the platform over the tank and set down the bucket. Her mother's problems had started on a track, at the site of a train derailment in which she'd been mentoring Kira's father on how to maintain order during mass casualty events. A little girl with red hair and mismatched socks, who later turned out to be a malevolent's vessel, had attached herself to Sarah's energy, thus triggering the chain reaction that had led to the destruction of the original Establishment. Maybe Jonathon had been right: as long as creatures like Kira existed, nothing was truly safe from harm. She was the inevitable damage.

She scanned the grid of enclosures and found Mason a short distance away, flagging the weak spots with glowing blue markers. All around him the walls were textured with spongy grey deposits and streaks of brownish-red blood. Altercations were common among malevolents, and the smaller ones—the losers—always paid the ultimate price.

"Galloway," came a voice from the floor. Kira looked down and scowled. "Are we here to sightsee, or are we here to work?"

Stepping back from the railing, Kira lifted the bucket onto her elbow and descended the second ladder leading to the bottom of the tank. The floor was a patchwork of algae and other grime, most of it malevolent waste and the hardened remains of their last meal. Kira treaded lightly over the carnage, her field as heavy as a lead jacket around her shoulders. If she didn't behave, this was where she would end up. Without Mason, of course.

She removed the coarse brush from her utility belt, dipped it in the solution, and set to work on polishing a section of the floor. Bit by bit, the stain thinned out and disappeared, revealing the icy black water and shadowy forms circling in a bottomless pool beneath the glass. Kira sawed at the residue until her hands burned. This should've been Dean's job, not hers. If he was so afraid of malevolents, why hadn't Ansel seen it fit to make *him* spend hours staring into their bloodshot eyes? The more audacious ones even pounded on the barrier, sending shockwaves through Kira's field.

Sometime later, a familiar voice brought her senses back into focus. The malevolents had given up trying to intimidate her and were now scouring the obsidian depths in search of food.

"Hey, Kira," Mason called, resting his elbows on the platform railing. "You missed a spot."

"Oh, look. Another joker." She scrubbed harder, but couldn't erase the hostility from her voice.

"You know, if Jonathon gives you a hard time, you can always give him the bird."

"The bird?"

Mason held up his middle finger, much to Kira's chagrin.

She turned back to the stubborn blotch. "That doesn't look like a bird at all."

He laughed and lowered his hand. "Did you hear what happened to Dean?"

"I heard he was being dealt with, whatever that means."

"It means he got suspended. But that's not all." Mason caught her quizzical gaze. "He's being reassessed. If he fails assessment, he might be purged."

Kira paled. "Purged?"

Mason nodded at the drainage grate, hidden beneath a sheet of steel in the middle of the floor. Once Jonathon approved the repairs, a button on the enclosure's outer wall would allow him to slide the barrier aside, refill the tank with water, then temporarily remove the grate so the malevolents could be reintroduced to their environment. But the drainage system worked both ways: not only did it coax morally compromised creatures into the light, but it also condemned dangerous offenders to an eternity of darkness.

Kira scrambled away from the drain, spilling the contents of the bucket. She pictured Dean spinning in the vortex while Jonathon watched disinterestedly through the glass. Then she saw her own face in the churning filth as the water sucked her through the bars and spat her out the other side, where she would sink in six or seven pieces in an eternal freefall. The darkness was full of monsters; even the humans knew this.

Her eyes had gone red at the edges like the sky above Irae by the time Mason reached the bottom of the ladder. He could taste her fear from across the tank; it had a distinct smokiness to it—the scorched flesh variety, rather than the more pleasant redolence of burning wood.

She blinked quickly, pulling her field back into alignment as she stepped away from him.

"I'm sorry," Kira mumbled, glancing at the grate. "I… I saw something."

"What did you see?"

"Dean." It wasn't the whole truth, but it was all she was willing to tell, for now.

"Ah. That explains the smoke."

"Smoke?"

"Your presence gives off a… particular scent."

"Are you saying I smell bad?"

"No! Of course not."

She stooped over the bucket and shook out the remaining grit. Now that the vision had passed, she had just enough energy to muster a smile.

"You're a bad liar," she informed him, retrieving the brush from where it had fallen on the floor, "but a good friend."

As she turned toward the glass, Kira spotted Jonathon racing to the elevator. He paused to confer with another employee before stepping into the cylindrical pod and vanishing in an instant.

"Did you see that?" she asked.

Mason climbed the ladder and scanned the area for Jonathon's coworker.

"Hey, Colt," Mason called as the Catcher on the ground looked up from his tool belt. "What's the situation?"

"Not sure. Apparently, Jon got called up to dispatch."

"Did he say why?"

"He just said it was an emergency and to keep an eye on the two of you." Colt moved to the next tank. "Back to work, Massey."

Kira climbed out of the tank as well, leaving the bucket and brush at the bottom. Before he could think of a reason to stop her, Mason saw a blur of blue-streaked hair flying across the maze like a raven. He smirked, pleased to see Kira had finally taken his advice on something.

The space traffic control room was a hive of anxious deliberation, and Kira managed to sneak in unnoticed. She was able to see the docking bay from here, along with the fleet of teardrop-shaped vehicles awaiting repairs between missions. The Commander 3 was missing from the lineup—and the radars.

"Commander 3, this is Headquarters. Do you copy?"

The frenzy broke momentarily. When the pilot didn't respond, the dispatcher activated the microphone again and repeated his simple message.

"Commander 3, this is Headquarters. Do you copy?" There was another pause. Kira shrank deeper into the corner, watching to see what her mother would do. "Do you copy, Commander 3?"

Silence settled over the room as Ansel approached the controls. Reaching for one of the headsets, he cupped it over his ears and adjusted the specifications on one of the screens. His reflection in the window showed no signs of distress, aside from a subtle motion of his chin that Kira subconsciously imitated.

"Commander 3," the dispatcher said for the last time, "please copy." When his plea was met by empty air, he calmly removed the headset, turned to his superior, and shook his head.

Ansel braced his hands on the desk and stared out at the abyss. Somewhere in the button box of overlapping universes, ancient galaxies, and misplaced planets, a thread had been cut, leaving the crew unable to communicate with The Establishment. For all Kira knew, they'd encountered a cosmic storm, or perhaps the free-floating remnants of obsolete satellites that Mason said were common around heavily populated planets like Earth. These were friends of hers, fellow Hunters with names and stories who'd vanished into thin air—an extraordinary feat, considering there was no air in space.

After a minute, Ansel turned to Sarah. "Have Celeste draft a memo. The others deserve to know what happened."

"Sir, even we don't know what happened to the crew. They could be in a dead zone with no signal, or maybe their security system has been compromised in some way and they've suspended all non-essential functions."

"Communication is an essential function," the original dispatcher interjected. "Especially during emergencies."

A voice farther down the row added, "These spacecrafts were designed to withstand every natural and human-made threat imaginable: meteors, inclement weather, nuclear disasters, hostile encounters… and you're suggesting that the crew voluntarily turned off their comms due to a security breach?"

"They might have, if the breach occurred internally." The focus of the conversation shifted to Jonathon, standing off to the side with his hands in his pockets. From Kira's vantage point, he looked more like a shy child than the resident expert on malevolent behaviour.

He continued. "July 14th, 1872: The Commander 7 crash-landed on Jupiter's largest moon, Ganymede, claiming all six crew members. We received a series of distress calls prior to impact—Crimson Alarms, which can only be triggered by negative energy in the cockpit—and lost contact shortly after."

Kira studied her Keepsake in thought. When danger was near, the stone turned red—a much smaller and more benign version of the Crimson Alarm, which signaled that catastrophe was imminent.

The Commander 7 served as a cautionary tale to Hunters-in-training: a reminder to check their equipment for signs of wear and tear, and always, always lock the doors.

"Did we receive a Crimson Alarm?" Ansel asked, facing the main dispatcher.

"No."

"Then let's not assume the worst-case scenario. Do we know where the crew was headed?"

The subordinate hovered over the controls, and soon a holographic projection appeared above one of the tracking pads. As she watched the planet turn, Kira felt something akin to an electric shock pass through her essence. Was it fear? Excitement? She couldn't be sure, but in that moment, one thing became blindingly clear: she had to find the crew, and quickly.

"Samoia," she whispered. Another shock; the planet was speaking to her—screaming, it would seem. Even after the image faded, Kira couldn't look away. If she had, then she would've noticed Mason lingering in the doorway, his face wrinkled with worry as her eyes slowly clouded over.

The uptick in energy prompted Sarah to turn around. "Kira, what are you doing here?"

"I asked Colt to keep an eye on both of them," Jonathon supplied, acknowledging Mason with a sidelong glare. "Clearly, I need better assistance."

"What's going on?" Mason asked, stepping into the room.

"Nothing that's of any concern to either of you. Now, please return to your posts." Sarah turned back to the controls, but was surprised to find Ansel's attention elsewhere.

"It's all right," he said, surprising them all, "they can stay." Moving closer to his young recruits, Ansel explained, "It appears we've lost contact with the crew aboard the Commander 3. We believe they may have crash-landed in enemy territory not far from here." He paused, awaiting Kira's reaction. "How would you feel about flying over Samoia?"

"I'd be honoured," she replied, standing up a little straighter. "When do I leave?"

"As soon as possible. But you'll need a partner."

Kira deflated. No one ever volunteered to go to Samoia: the Black Widow of the cosmos, famous for its web of deception that made mountain ranges out of smoke and turned empty air into brick walls. Fly too low, and the ground would meet you halfway—even if it hadn't existed a second before. Still, she wasn't about to let an opportunity like this slip away. She was a Hunter; chasing monsters was in her blood—even if that monster happened to be a planet.

"I'll do it," Mason said, meeting Kira's eyes across the room. "I've been on at least a dozen reconnaissance missions. This one won't be any different."

"Wrong. This is Samoia. *Everything* about this planet is different." The dispatcher spun away from the desk and frowned at what he considered to be two careless children looking to cause trouble. "I've been doing this job for close to a thousand years. I know every speck of space dust from here to the edge of nowhere, and nothing comes close to Samoia in terms of pretending to be something it isn't—except you, Kira."

Sarah's voice turned frigid. "Don't talk to my daughter that way. Or any of my employees, for that matter."

"We're just trying to help," Mason said with considerably more heat. "You won't find the crew from behind your desk. You need to get out there and pound the pavement—or the space dust, as you say."

Turning to one of the employees Kira had seen inspecting the Commander 2 on the day of their return, Ansel said, "Tell your team we need a spotter fueled and flight-ready by the time Kira and Mr. Massey arrive in the hangar. In the meantime, Sarah can show you both to the dressing rooms."

Kira was humming like a streetlight. The Samoian malevolents had perfected the art of camouflage, more than anywhere else. But what really captured her interest were the illusions: massive, seething mirages that sprang up in areas previously occupied by nature, mystifying even the most seasoned pilots. Still, if she could complete this mission, then maybe it would compel Ansel to rethink her penalty.

"So it's settled," he said as the activity around them resumed. "Kira and Mason will fly over Samoia and get a visual on the Commander 3. Unless there are any objections, I say we proceed."

"I have an objection," Sarah said firmly.

"You can't be serious," Kira snapped. "Why do you always have to ruin things for me?"

"I haven't ruined anything for you. But this is Samoia we're talking about. If it were any other planet, any other mission, I'd have no objections."

"If it were any other planet, it wouldn't matter."

Sarah exchanged glances with Ansel, then walked toward the door.

"A word with you, please?" Sarah said as she passed. Kira turned and followed her mother into the hallway, leaving Mason standing in the doorway while Ansel conferred with his staff.

"Look, I'm sorry," Kira said, struggling to match Sarah's confident strides. "What was I supposed to do? Stand there and say nothing?"

"Actually, you were supposed to be in the basement. But that's beside the point."

They rounded a corner. Despite the abundance of light, Sarah's expression was shadowy and mysterious, causing Kira to take a step back.

"Why do you want to go to Samoia so badly?" Sarah asked, her voice shedding some of its acrimony. "There will be other missions."

"I can't explain it, really. It's like… a shock."

"A shock?"

"That's what I felt, when Hector pulled up the projection. It was like suddenly everything made sense and I finally understood why I'm different." Kira closed her eyes, picturing the ball of energy lighting up the control room. "Samoia wants to be like the other planets, but it's not. It's dangerous, and anyone who tries to get close to it ends up wishing they hadn't."

"You're not dangerous," Sarah said softly, running her hand down Kira's arm; her skin was warm, but pale. On the outside, she looked exactly like every other Spirit Catcher—an angel without wings, a ghost without a grudge. Inside, though, she would always be half malevolent like her father, Gabe. That meant there was no arguing with her once she'd made up her mind.

"I have to do this," Kira continued with considerably more force. "It's not just another mission for me—it's a defining moment in my career. Just like defeating the malevolents was a defining moment in yours."

Sarah nodded, surrendering her side of the fight. "In that case, head down to the dressing room and get suited up. Damien hates to be kept waiting."

Awakening

"Anything yet?" Kira asked, maintaining her vice-like grip on the controls as the spotter glided through a patch of clouds.

"Nothing." Mason panned his gaze over the valley. He'd barely looked up from the radar since they'd left The Establishment, but the clockwise rotation of the scanner was making him cross-eyed. "I see two of you though."

Kira tensed her jaw; now wasn't the time for jokes. She glanced at the radar nestled in the centre of the console, but the trailing line of green detected no irregularities in the landscape—or at least, nothing of the intergalactic type. "Regular" wasn't a word she could confidently use in a place like Samoia.

Mason stared at the strip of glass between his feet. The valley bubbled like a pot of hot soup, spewing rock formations and forests that would have taken centuries to grow on planet Earth. With any luck, they'd find the Commander 3 before Samoia submerged it at the bottom of a lake.

The headset crackled. "Do you have a visual on the subject, Recon One?"

"Negative on the visual," Mason replied. "Headquarters, could you please relay the crew's last known coordinates?"

"Third upper quadrant, fifteen miles south of Distinction 9."

"Distinction 9?" He scoured the horizon for a vertical rod pinpointing the geographical centre of Samoia's top-crust plateau. "Are you sure?"

"Yes, Recon One. We received a ping from D9 less than an hour ago."

Failing to find the blue beacon, Mason leaned back in his seat. "Copy that, Headquarters. We'll report back if we see anything."

"Maybe they aren't even down there," Kira suggested. "What if we have the wrong planet? Or the wrong galaxy? Ansel could be testing us."

"Ansel's already lost six of his employees. Sending us to the wrong galaxy in a spacecraft that only has enough fuel for one round trip would be a waste of his resources." Mason glimpsed her face. "We need to descend."

"We have orders against flying too low."

"If they want a visual, then they're getting a visual." Mason gently tipped the joystick forward, guiding the spacecraft closer to the ground.

"Mason, pull up," Kira urged. "Stay above the illusions."

"We're at forty-five thousand feet, Kira. We have plenty of room to spare." Pressing a button on his headset, Mason spoke into the microphone. "Headquarters, this is Recon One over Samoia. We're at forty-five thousand feet and still have no visual. Seeking permission to descend."

"Permission granted, Recon One. Watch your altitude."

"Roger that." He flashed her a reassuring grin. "See? Nothing to worry about."

"I still think we're too low."

"Look, if the crew's gone under the radar, this is the only hope we have of finding them. Just trust me."

"It's not you I don't trust. It's this planet."

They dropped again, this time to thirty-nine thousand feet. On the ground, a roaring river evaporated in seconds, leaving a parched plateau in its wake. Pillars of clay rose from the earth as if a pair of invisible hands was controlling their shape. The clay towers hardened, gaining four faces each. Windows shimmered into view, layering the concrete façade with thousands of blue-grey eyes. The eyes of a monster.

"Do you ever get the feeling you're being watched?" Mason asked humourlessly.

"Aren't we all?" The illusive skyscrapers fired needles of sunlight into their cockpit as they passed. As soon as she could see clearly again, Kira checked their altitude: twenty-seven thousand feet and falling. She looked over at the radar, but it was dishearteningly blank.

"What's the situation, Recon One?" came a voice from inside their headsets.

"Still no visual. Altitude is now twenty-three thousand feet." Mason fiddled with the controls and added, "If we don't see them in the next two minutes, I'm ascending."

Kira nodded. An imaginary city was probably the tallest obstacle they'd encounter out here (whipping up a mountain peak took too much time), but until she could look up and see pure blue skies overhead, she would have to remain vigilant.

As the spotter careened around a craggy slope, a glimmer of light drew Kira's eyes downward. If what she felt in the control room had been an electric shock, then the feeling she experienced now was more like being struck by lightning.

"There it is," she exclaimed. Her excitement quickly diminished as trees broke through the dirt like massive emerald umbrellas, blotting the Commander from view.

"Headquarters, this is Recon One. We have a visual on the subject," Mason reported. "Coordinates are 49° 6.2 / 73° 9.1."

"Nice work, Recon One. Search and rescue have been dispatched."

"We don't have time to wait for search and rescue," Kira said as the foliage spread and thickened. "We'll have lost them again by the time help arrives."

"Headquarters, we're losing sight of the subject. Seeking permission to land."

This time, it wasn't a dispatcher that replied, but Ansel himself.

"Permission to land denied, Recon One. This is a reconnaissance mission, Mr. Massey, not a rescue mission. I repeat: you do not have permission to land."

"We're losing them," Kira said.

"I'm circling back." Mason said into the microphone, "Headquarters, how soon can you get a team out here?"

"Twenty minutes. The team is assembling in the hangar as we speak."

"We don't have twenty minutes," Mason mumbled. Glancing at Kira, he nodded and said, "I'm putting her down. Someone needs to check on the crew."

"Search and rescue are inbound, Recon One."

"Copy that. Please be advised we'll be landing in less than two minutes."

"Recon One, you do not have permission to land. Please stand by for search and rescue."

He covered his microphone and turned to his partner. "Hey, Kira?"

She looked at him.

"I'm glad you're here. If there's anyone who's cut out for Samoia, it's you." He reached for the joystick and aimed the two-person spacecraft at the ground, sending their instruments into a frenzy.

"Where should we land?" Kira asked as they stabilized at a thousand feet.

"Somewhere there are no trees." Mason looked over his shoulder as they flew back toward the downed Commander. "Maybe that field over there?"

"If the trees close in on us, we won't be able to get airborne in an emergency. Maybe we should wait for backup."

"We don't have time to wait, and neither does the crew."

Despite her reservations, Kira nodded and monitored the controls. They were now five hundred feet off the ground and had an unimpeded view of the horizon to the north. Behind them, they could make out the dome of the Commander's cockpit through a gap in the wall of trees.

When Kira faced forward again, Mason was tinkering with the radar and oblivious to the altitude alarm beeping furiously on the panel between them.

"If we end up in a forest, at least it'll give us some protection from lurking malevolents," he said.

"Maybe," Kira said, "or maybe it'll make it easier for them to sneak up on us."

"Doubtful. Samoia is crawling with prey. Why come after us?"

"Well for one thing, we're trespassing on their planet."

"That seems like a pretty benign reason to attack."

"Since when have the malevolents ever needed a reason?"

"Kira, relax. The only hunters on this planet are——"

"Mason!"

He tore his gaze from the radar as a spire materialized in their path. Mason jerked the joystick sideways, narrowly missing the illusion. The spotter veered violently along its warped trajectory, triggering multiple alarms and making Kira grind her teeth. Moments later, a mountain broke the surface of the earth, shaking off the dirt and trees as it rose sharply on their left. Mason leaned the controls in the opposite direction; they banked hard, but not soon enough to avoid the spotter's wing connecting with the tip of Samoia's stone tooth.

Crippled by the mountain's blow, the spotter staggered into a tailspin. Ribbons of thick, black smoke wrapped around its damaged wing as they hurdled toward the ground. A dense carpet of trees obliterated the once barren field as they bobbed over the forest, buoyed by a strong wind and whatever remained of their energy.

"Headquarters, this is Recon One," Mason said as the spotter sputtered into a nosedive. "We've struck an obstacle and are experiencing full system failure. Attempting forced landing three miles north-east of aforementioned subject."

Mason managed to gain a shred of control over the failing spacecraft. The spotter lurched above the canopy before the engine died and they dropped again. The spacecraft crashed through the blanket of foliage and skipped along the forest floor, snapping trees like matches before eventually sliding to a stop at the base of a large tree with smooth grey bark and thorny purple flowers.

The last of the alarms pinged softly, then the cockpit went quiet.

Kira lifted her head and gazed at the debris littering the controls. The cawing of a bird shattered the silence as she fumbled for the radio and pressed the button to speak.

"Headquarters, this is Recon One," she said, her voice cracking. "Do you copy?"

Kira waited. Beside her, Mason was upright but unconscious. She tried to wake him using her free hand, but recoiled from the pain of the busted shoulder bar against her skin.

"Headquarters," she said again, more insistently this time, "this is Recon One. Do you copy?"

Kira lowered the radio and surveyed her surroundings. The field where they'd been planning to land had transformed into a jungle, complete with vines as thick as her arm and the rich, sweet fragrance of decay. A symphony of chirps, chatters, and whistles enveloped their crumpled spacecraft like fog, adding to the confusion she felt trying to establish her location. Growing desperate, Kira once again lifted the radio to her mouth and activated the microphone.

"Headquarters, if you can hear me, please copy."

Static flooded the line. She stared at the device as the weight of their solitude settled over her. When her inquiry was met with empty air, she set the radio back in its cradle and turned her attention to the next problem: exiting the wreckage in one piece.

She struggled to free herself, pushing against the misshapen shoulder bar to no avail. The restraint had been crushed when the roof caved in, and there was no way to unpin herself from the collapsed bubble without first removing the tree branch. She knew how to manipulate objects in her environment the way ghosts did in movies, but that took more energy than she had right now. Unless she borrowed some from Mason.

Kira stretched her left hand out as far as it would go. The Keepsake served many functions—among them, the ability to transfer energy from one Catcher to another. All she had to do was hold her band against his, and the copper conduits would syphon the electricity out of Mason's ring and into hers.

She winced as the pressure in her shoulder culminated in a burst of pain. A cry ripped from her vocal cords as she slammed her head back against the seat and belted out the first four-letter word that came to mind. Mason was right: she *did* feel better.

"Okay," she whispered to herself, centring her field as best she could under the circumstances. "It's okay—you can do this." She'd gotten lucky: rather than hanging at his side, his left hand had landed in his lap. If this was one of Ansel's tests, Kira was determined to pass with flying colours.

She leaned sideways again, grabbed Mason's hand, and squeezed his fingers to activate the stone. His Keepsake cast a golden glow on the smashed screens. The incoming energy had an intoxicating effect on her—so intoxicating, in fact, that Kira began to see red.

She dropped Mason's hand and stared in horror at her own. What if she'd taken too much from him? What if this whole trip had been nothing more than an excuse to purge her from The Establishment's catalogue, and the crew wasn't actually stranded, but waiting patiently for her to wander into their trap? What if Jonathon had been right all along?

"No," Kira told herself. "You're not a monster. You are *not* a monster." Mason would be okay. He had to be.

But enough of this. She came here to find the crew, and she wasn't leaving without them.

Kira channeled her attention on the broken branch jutting through the spotter's ceiling. It didn't budge, so she concentrated on moving just one leaf to start. Her energy shifted, and before long, the green appendage fluttered in the artificial breeze. The splintered limb rocked under her influence, and like a sliver from a fingertip, slowly slid free.

Next, Kira applied her strength to the restraints, beginning with the metal bar draped across her torso. Lifting it over her head, she unclasped the nylon belt across her lap before tearing off the straps around her shins. She attempted to stand, but didn't make it far before a patch of shadow dimmed her vision and she sank back into the seat.

Kira lifted her arm and found pure, black energy oozing from a hole between her ribs. Still dazed from the impact, she used her fingers to wipe the blood-like substance from around the puncture wound and discovered a dull, red light pulsing in the darkness of her shell. Her essence. Its glow was weak—a sure sign of damage, Kira thought abstractly, looking around for something to staunch the bleeding. The vision in her right eye was getting fuzzy and grey like moldy bread, but she shook her head and forced herself to focus.

Having identified the first aid kit strapped to the wall at the spacecraft's rear, Kira grappled to a standing position. She paused a moment to collect herself before maneuvering the cockpit to reach the white box containing everything she'd need to bind the wound.

The kit landed on the floor with a noisy clatter as Kira dropped to her knees and rummaged through the mess. Finding the gauze, she tore the package open and lifted the hem of her shirt. She covered the hole with several layers of the absorbent white fabric before securing it in place with a generous length of cling gauze. Satisfied with the pressure on her ribs, she leaned against the nearest wall and fought to stay conscious.

In the end, the blackness won.

●

The plaintive cry of a wolf jolted Kira from her slumber. Pale ivory light poured into the cockpit, illuminating the bits of broken glass ornamenting the controls. Outside, the rainforest had transformed into a temperate forest, complete with prickly patches of lichen and stout green conifers with long, silky needles dangling like tassels from their bows. An owl hooted in the distance, and Kira, alarmed by its forlorn statement, leapt inelegantly to her feet, only to be dragged to her knees by an energy field that hadn't yet recalibrated.

She waited for her form to find its equilibrium before attempting to stand again. She searched the cockpit, expecting to find Mason still strapped into his seat, but the restraints had all been undone and he was nowhere to be seen.

Kira stumbled out into the night. The air was cool and the sky was clear and bright, frosted with stars from edge to edge. The Establishment was out there somewhere, teeming behind the veil that separated this life from the next. If Ansel was watching her, the least he could do was give her a sign.

The universe barely blinked. Kira shuddered as a knot formed in her core. So *this* was how it felt to be homesick: like she was caving in on herself, getting smaller and smaller until the loneliness swallowed her whole. She wanted her mother. Mason's presence would satisfy her need for comfort until the family was reunited, but first, Kira had to find him.

Compared to the spotter, the Commander was relatively unscathed. Its emergency door stood open, the ramp half-sunken in a murky puddle. The abandoned cockpit was swimming in shadows, but none that resembled danger as far as Kira could see. She kept her distance all the same, eyeing the water apprehensively. Malevolents were amphibious, and water provided the perfect disguise, especially at night. Kira scavenged through the litterfall for something to toss into the puddle. She unearthed a small rock, which made a hollow popping sound as it sank beneath the surface. Ripples radiated across the moonlit mirror, then faded as silence returned to the woods.

She raised her hand. Light streamed from her fingertips as she stepped toward the spacecraft and called softly into the darkness, "Mason?"

Nothing had jumped out at her when she threw the stone, so Kira took her chances and waded into the ankle-deep pool. The beam traipsed over the empty seats and discarded headsets before settling on a trail of muddy boot prints along the floor.

"Mason?" Kira called again, climbing inside. "Anyone?"

The crew would've stayed with their vehicle, and yet there was no sign of them anywhere. The floor sloped sideways, and anything not secured to the walls had rolled into the corners, casting shadows that toyed with Kira's imagination. She followed the tracks through the hallways and chambers, keeping her light low to preserve her energy. Before long, a series of splatters appeared alongside the footprints. Blood stains. The decontamination bay lay straight ahead, supplying enough light to illuminate the handprint smeared across the glass door.

Kira shimmied through the opening. The footprints were fading, but the blood trail continued, leading her down another hallway and up a flight of stairs to a room filled with metal containers. Here, the shadows appeared to dance as she waved her hand from side to side, certain she was being watched.

The light died as she dropped her hand and groped for a path to safety. Her foot struck the corner of a crate. She fell forward as a burst of energy exploded above her head, raining snapshots of family camping trips, birthday parties, and swimming lessons onto the floor: the remains of Mason's orb.

Another streak of blue sailed through the air and connected with one of the containers. The second orb was fainter than the first and merely crumbled like a crushed cigarette, rather than generating shockwaves that might've flattened her if she was still standing. Nevertheless, when the memories landed on her skin, Kira cried out in pain as if every image was a piece of shrapnel.

"Mason, stop!" Kira lifted her head and stared at the wall of boxes shielding her partner from view.

A third orb began to form in Mason's grasp, but he clung tightly to his adolescence, frozen by the chill of a familiar voice in the darkness. "Kira?"

"Yes, it's me."

"Are you hurt?"

"No," she lied, lifting herself off the floor. "Are you?"

He opened his hand, disarming the blue grenade. It tumbled out of his fingers and rolled between his feet, casting a dull spotlight on the object protruding from his thigh.

"Yeah," Mason answered. "They got me."

"Who?"

"Not who—what." He stared at the quill, but couldn't summon his faculties long enough to remove it.

Kira faltered. "Malevolents?"

"Malevolents," he replied, closing his eyes.

She came around the corner slowly, unsure of what she'd find on the other side. Her light fell on Mason's pained expression first, and as she moved her hand down his form, the source of his suffering became clear.

"What happened?" Kira asked. "You were supposed to stay with the spotter until help arrived."

Mason grimaced and tried to sit up.

"I know," he rasped. "But I was worried about the crew. We didn't come all this way just to leave them out here."

He swallowed and gestured to the quill.

"I came here first, thinking they might have chosen to shelter in place. When I realized they'd left, I decided to expand my search. The landscape changed again before I could get to cover. That's when I found the malevolents… or rather, when they found me."

Mason planted his hands on the floor and boosted himself up. Once he was comfortable again, he continued.

"I diffused a couple of orbs. The smaller malevolents took off right away, but the alpha didn't give up that easily. He circled me a few times and would've probably bitten me, if he'd gotten that close. Instead, he got me with one of his quills." Mason patted his leg for emphasis. "I finally managed to scare him off and limp to the Commander. I considered returning to the spotter, but didn't know if I could make it that far in my condition."

"Can't you just remove the quill and bind the wound?"

Mason shook his head. "I tried. It won't come out."

Kira crouched and examined Mason's leg more closely. The quill—or at least the part of it she could see—had a sleek, bone-like exterior and a rough, blackened root. The poison dripping from the tip had caused the flesh surrounding the entry site to blister and peel. Kira wrapped her hand around the quill, recoiling when it singed her skin.

"Damn it! Why is it so hot?"

"I don't know. It did it to me, too."

"But there has to be a way. It can't stay in there."

"I'm sure there is," Mason mumbled as she rifled through the containers for something to cover her hand. "I just don't know what it is."

Kira returned to his side and wrapped an old cloth around the quill. She took hold a second time and pulled, but the pointed appendage lodged itself more deeply into Mason's leg, causing him to cry out in pain.

"Please, just stop it," he growled, "stop before you make it worse."

"I don't understand. Is it barbed?"

"No."

"So why won't it come out?"

"I don't know. It's like it has a mind of its own." Mason massaged his thigh, but the soothing motion brought no relief. The humans had a saying that laughter was the best medicine. A chuckle was the most he could manage in his state, but Kira didn't join in.

"What's so funny?" she snapped.

"When I was a kid, we had a dog," Mason started, his smile growing as she stared at him. Kira was dumbfounded, and it was hilarious. "A beagle, named Duchess. We took her camping every summer, and one year she picked a fight with a porcupine. She got a quill, a small one, stuck in her face and the vet said to let it work its way through. I was thinking maybe I should do the same, you know? Let this poison-tipped souvenir travel through my leg and out the other side. Of course, there's the minor detail of my femur standing in the way…"

"Work its way through? But that could take hours."

"Weeks," Mason corrected, folding his hands in his lap as if he intended to sit here and prove it. "But I'll be out of energy long before that happens." He scoffed. "On the bright side, at least I won't die."

His laughter became uncontrollable. He clutched his ribs, which had begun to ache, and thanked God—no, thanked Ansel—that his focus had been momentarily diverted from his leg.

"Seriously, *what* is so funny?" The angrier Kira got, the harder Mason laughed.

"Laughter… is… the best medicine," he sputtered.

She arched a brow. "Another one of your brilliant sayings, I'm guessing?"

"Do you like it?"

"No, it's stupid. Laughter isn't the best medicine—*medicine* is the best medicine." She sobered. "You need medicine."

"Yes, I do. So head to the cockpit and try the radio again. There has to be someone out there. *Anyone.*"

Kira hesitated. She recalled radioing Headquarters from the spotter's cockpit, only to be reminded of why her mother had been so resistant to the mission in the first place. Samoia was the unkindest of planets, and she had a particular hankering for amateur pilots with grandiose intentions. Even if the forest cleared at the exact moment that search and rescue was doing a flyby, there was no guarantee they'd be seen, and especially not in the dark. Still, she had nothing to lose by trying.

She threw one last glance at her companion, then turned and raced back to the Commander's cockpit. Once there, she swept aside the piles of paper until she uncovered the radio. Wrenching it out of its cradle, she put the device to her mouth and hoped for the best.

"Headquarters, this is Kira Galloway. I'm in the cockpit of the Commander 3 and the crew is MIA. If you can hear me, please copy."

There was a long stretch of silence, but nonetheless, she persisted.

"Headquarters, this is Kira Galloway calling from the Commander 3. Requesting immediate assistance."

She looked up and froze. Through a break in the trees, she spotted the triangular configuration of lights belonging to a low-flying search and rescue craft. Tree leaves fluttered as it hummed over the woods, bathing the forest in bright blue light.

Kira stumbled out of the Commander and trudged through the snow to reach the clearing. She shouted and waved her arms, but the spacecraft had already aimed its searchlight elsewhere.

She needed more light. More energy.

She needed to harness the power of Samoia.

Kira studied her Keepsake, smoothing her thumb over the reddish swirls in the band. The planet had been speaking to her long before she'd set foot on its soil—and now, she was about to send a message back.

She knelt on the ground and placed both hands on the ice. Heat streamed from her fingers in bright orange rivulets, melting the crystallized blanket until a cushion of leaves and moss softened under her touch. The ground carried a positive charge; she could feel every molecule of moisture and clump of dirt stinging her to the bone. Here she was, the message said: Kira Galloway, half Spirit Catcher, half malevolent, filled with fire and an essence that only discharged negative energy. It was the perfect storm—the ideal conditions for lightning to strike.

Kira gathered her strength, then pressed the band of her ring against the earth. A spark jumped from the copper path, hit the ground, and zigzagged back up to the sky, infusing the clouds with a brilliant flash of amaranth. A crack of thunder accompanied the bolt, echoing off the trees with such force that icicles fell from their branches like missiles from a warplane. Message received.

Kira rocked back on her heels and gazed up at the sky. After a few seconds, the triangular lights returned. They hovered above the trees as the search beam completed its rotation, and soon the craft was carefully lowered to the ground.

Sarah appeared wearing an orange jumpsuit, her dark blonde hair yanked into a tight bun and her hands clutching a robust black emergency kit. Kira struggled through the dense snow and threw her arms around her mother's neck.

"Thank goodness you're okay," Sarah said as Kira buried her face in her shoulder. "When we lost contact with the spotter, I made Ansel put me on the search and rescue team, even though the only things we had to go on were your last coordinates." She stood back, looking her daughter over. "Are you hurt?"

"I'm fine. But Mason needs help." Kira indicated the metallic shell in the distance. "The crew's not in there. He got attacked by a malevolent while looking for them and hid in one of the storage rooms."

"When did this happen?"

"I don't know. I passed out after we crashed and when I woke up, Mason was gone."

Glancing at Damien, Sarah picked up her kit and strode past Kira to the Commander. Once inside, Kira led the way to the storage room.

"Mason?" Kira said before she opened the door. She shone her light on his face, which was pale, sunken, and beaded with sweat. Alarmed by how rapidly he'd deteriorated in only a few minutes, she stood frozen on the threshold until Sarah arrived and motioned for Damien to move some of the boxes.

"Kira said you were attacked," Sarah said as she bent over Mason's leg. "Were you bitten too?"

Mason swallowed audibly and shook his head. His eyes were bloodshot and his lips were chapped, but he kept his gaze trained on Kira, towering above the wall of supply crates.

Sarah reached for her bag. Undoing the zipper, she flipped up the lid and produced several syringes from the elastic loops lining the interior. These she laid on the floor next to her patient before turning back to the case to hunt for a plastic bag and a pair of metal tweezers.

Mason eyed the supplies warily, but didn't have the strength to inquire about their various functions.

"Shine a light here, Kira," Sarah said as Damien squatted on Mason's other side. When Kira didn't react, Sarah angled toward her daughter and raised her voice. "Kira. Your light, please."

Kira shook off her stupor as she held her hand over the quill.

"Okay," Sarah said, "now let's take a look."

She removed the soiled towel and set it aside. Her face scrunching in concentration, she inspected the flesh around the quill before reaching for the smallest of the three syringes. Kira lowered her hand as Sarah slid back the hem of Mason's pants and pierced his skin with the tip of the needle.

"What is that?" Kira asked.

"Neutralizer, to prevent the infection from spreading." With the plunger fully depressed, Sarah withdrew the needle, capped it, and chucked it into the bag.

"I tried to pull the quill out, but it lodged itself in deeper. And it got really hot, hence the towel."

Sarah reached for a second, slightly thicker syringe.

"Samoian malevolent quills are designed to remain in the victim's body until all the poison is administered," she explained as Mason's eyelids began to droop. The crinkle of the plastic bag jolted him back to awareness. "If you could remove them by force, they'd be useless."

"So how do we get it out?"

"Simple: we cut off the poison supply." Sarah popped the translucent plastic cap off the needle and scouted Mason's leg for the most appropriate place to insert it.

"This is freezing serum," she said of the pale blue liquid in the syringe. "The way it works is by entering the tip of the quill and inhibiting the flow of poison. Once all the poison has been frozen, the quill will shrivel and become loose, at which time we'll be able to extract it." Sarah glimpsed Mason's face. "Ready?"

He nodded. Across from him, Kira did the same.

Sarah plunged the needle into Mason's thigh, and the blue solution bulged beneath his skin. The serum zipped into the quill, and soon it became pasty and brittle. By the time the root crumbled, Sarah had the tweezers in one hand and the plastic bag in the other.

She deposited the quill into the bag and sealed it with her thumb and forefinger, leaving a black hole in the middle of Mason's leg.

"We'll take this back to the lab," she said to Damien. Tucking the specimen into her kit, Sarah reached for the third and final syringe before addressing Mason again.

"Why is he shivering?" Kira asked, eyeing her partner as he trembled uncontrollably.

"It's a side effect of the serum. We'll worry about that in a minute." Exposing the last needle, Sarah said to Mason, "This is to rebuild the compromised tissue. I can't promise it won't hurt."

Within seconds of administering the shot, the rotted flesh receded and Mason began to whimper—softly at first, then more insistently as the clear fluid entered his muscle. A growl of agony escaped his lips as the tremors intensified. Damien squeezed his shoulder while

Sarah applied pressure to his ankle, immobilizing his leg until the last of the solution had taken effect.

After a couple of minutes, Sarah slid back Mason's pant leg to find the skin clean and unblemished, but cold to the touch.

"You're all fixed, soldier," Sarah said as she patted his knee. To Damien, she said, "Find him a blanket. He'll need to rest for a while, but I don't expect he'll experience any long-term complications."

Sarah collected her bag from the floor as Damien uncovered a thermal blanket from one of the boxes and spread it over Mason's form. A short distance away, Kira stood quietly, her hand still illuminated as she gazed at her partner's face.

"Kira?" She looked at her mother, who smiled and said, "Damien and I are going to go lay some tethers so we don't lose either the Commander or our search craft. Keep an eye on Mason, okay?"

Kira waited until the other Catchers were out of sight, then took a seat on the floor beside him.

"I'm sorry," she whispered as he continued to shake beneath the reflective cover. "I should've been with you when you confronted those malevolents."

"I'm glad you weren't. We have enough to worry about as it is." Mason looked at her. "Do you regret it?"

"You mean coming to Samoia?" Kira shrugged and studied her hands. "I don't know. Do you?"

"Yes and no. I'd rather be stuck in the Commander 3 with you than taking orders from Dean."

"His judgment can't be any worse than mine."

Mason smirked. "Dean picked a fight with a bear and lost. I don't trust his judgment on anything." Running a hand down his face, he nestled deeper into the pocket of warmth—something he wasn't used to feeling—and asked, "By the way, you didn't happen to borrow some of my energy in the spotter, did you?"

Kira's eyes widened. "You were conscious?"

"Barely, but yeah. I felt your hand around mine at one point, but I thought that if you knew I was awake, you'd let go."

She steered her focus elsewhere. For a malevolent, she sure felt a lot of shame. Not that she'd ever hurt Mason intentionally, but being on Samoia had proven that even control was nothing more than a cruel illusion.

"I almost didn't," Kira admitted, avoiding Mason's gaze. "Your energy… it was… like a drug. Once it hit me, I… I started wanting more and more. I knew that if I didn't let go soon, I might be stuck here—alone."

"It's okay to let go, Kira. You don't have to hold onto something just because it's familiar to you." He added, "As for the drugs, well… I think I finally understand why Ansel sent me here."

"But he didn't send you. You volunteered."

"And he allowed it because there's a lesson in all this—something I couldn't learn anywhere else, and certainly not on Earth." Mason smiled. "I had to learn to let go."

"And what's my lesson?"

"I can't tell you that. You have to figure it out on your own." Lifting the edge of the blanket, Mason beckoned her with a subtle tilt of his head. "In the meantime, you can work on repaying some of that energy."

Kira slithered in beside him. Her hand found his under the thin covering, and as it did, he stopped shivering.

"Better?" she asked as his Keepsake gleamed like a newly minted coin.

"Much. Almost too good." Mason removed their fingers from under the blanket and stared at her stone wavering in the darkness. "It's fluttering—like a butterfly."

"You mean like the butterflies you claimed to have in your nonexistent stomach?" Kira teased.

"Exactly." He cupped his hand around her cheek. "Do you want to feel them too?"

Confused but electrified by his touch, Kira nodded tensely. Mason's lips locked onto hers, and for the first time since she sparked into being, a shiver raced up her spine.

The Saguaro's Shadow

Kira emerged from the Commander to find an autumn lake studded with crystals of early morning sunlight. She scanned the shoreline for signs of trouble, but the only movement came from the wind, which ruffled the surface of the water while the trees blushed copper in the distance.

Thankful for her solitude, she knelt at the water's edge and cupped a handful of it in her palms. She cleansed the dirt from her skin before unwinding the nest of hair and letting the liberated strands fly away from her neck. Her shoulder still sported a black stain where the restraint had dug into her flesh, and even the cool caress of the wind made her eyes burn from the pain.

Kira's face scrunched into a tight knot; she wouldn't be caught crying over a bruise when the crew was missing, her mother was planning her most dangerous rescue mission to date, and Mason was partly disabled from his injuries. Only children cried for such trivial reasons, and Kira didn't want to be seen that way anymore: as someone who still needed her mother. Her mother: a woman who'd come back from the dead five times, conceived Kira in a body she was merely borrowing, and raised her in a place where seeing ghosts was anything but spooky. It wasn't until Kira saw her reflection again that she realized her tears originated from laughter, rather than sorrow. Mason had been right about this, too—not that she would ever admit it.

After the pain had worn off, he'd settled into something resembling sleep. As the hours passed, she'd sat beside him in that cluttered storage room and tried to imagine who he'd been before his death: where he'd lived, what he'd thought of his parents, and other questions she'd never bothered to ask. The Living didn't talk about death because it was too scary; the Dead didn't talk about life because it was too sad. But Mason told her everything anyway, so she wouldn't feel left out—and so she'd be prepared when her time came to return to the light.

When Mason had opened his eyes, Kira asked, "What were your parents like?"

He'd folded his hands in his lap. At times, he reminded her of a wise elder on a mountaintop, perfectly at peace with his surroundings.

"They had a lot of… expectations," Mason had begun. "My father was a wealthy man, and my mother believed that anything less than perfect was failure. They were determined to control me by any means necessary, and drugs were the only way I could think of to cope—the only solution to their bullying and control tactics."

"But the drugs destroyed you," Kira had argued, not quite sure she understood his logic.

Mason had held her gaze, his expression sober. "I know. But it got me away from them… very far away."

"Kira? Is everything all right?" Sarah asked.

Kira turned away from the water to find a stone-faced figure standing on the shore, her orange uniform assimilating seamlessly with the landscape. She stood up, recovering her composure. "I'm fine."

Sarah smiled and picked her way down the slope.

"Mason's leg is healing nicely," she said. "I moved him into a recharging chamber to help him align his field, so hopefully he'll be well enough to join the search for the crew before it gets dark again."

"This is my fault, isn't it? Because I wanted to come here. You said it was dangerous, and I refused to listen."

"Fault isn't the word I'd use. Mason's injury is a consequence of a poorly thought-out action. Every planet is dangerous, but not nearly as dangerous as a stubborn mind." Sarah cracked a thin smile at her daughter. "Mind you, stubbornness is a double-edged sword: it cuts through common sense, but also the fear of failure."

"I am scared though. I'm scared for Mason."

"Mason will be fine. The crew, on the other hand, may not last another day here. The longer they go without contacting The Establishment, the less viable their energy becomes."

"I'll do whatever it takes to find them," Kira said.

"That's the part that worries me."

Sarah tore her eyes away. The lake was gone. The leaves were gone. Even the stones saw no reason to linger. She'd spent decades studying this planet, but there seemed to be no explanation for the changing seasons. Samoia was impulse personified—and it had conjured a lake strictly for Kira's benefit, so she could see herself reflected in the scenery.

As if to prove her unpredictability, Kira burst out laughing again. She clamped a hand over her side as a sharp pain struck her ribs, reminding her of why she'd left the Commander in the first place.

"Why didn't you tell me you were hurt?" Sarah asked.

"Because," Kira replied, keeping pressure on the wound, "I can take care of myself."

Sarah reeled her daughter in for a closer look. When she raised a hand to the tender flesh, Kira instinctively winced and pulled away.

"That's not a malevolent scratch, is it?" Sarah asked.

"It happened during the crash. And so did this." Kira tugged the collar of her white shirt away from her neck, revealing the damage to her shoulder. "It's not as bad as it looks."

"Can you move your arm?"

"Well enough."

Sarah turned her attention back to the wound in Kira's side. Her field felt weak in this spot, like a sheet of plastic stretched over a broken window.

"You need to realign yourself," she said as Kira smoothed her shirt back into place. "Once we return to The Establishment, I'll have one of my colleagues reboot your energy—but since that's not possible right now, you need to focus on redistributing whatever protection you have so you don't seem so appealing to malevolents."

"I'm okay, mom. Stop worrying."

Sarah shifted her focus back to the Commander. The night before, she and Damien had walked the perimeter to scout for clues as to the crew's whereabouts. When the forest transformed into rolling hills, they'd taken advantage of the elevated terrain to expand their search into outlying regions. Dismayed by their lack of success, they'd returned to camp and deliberated until sunrise, poring over portable scanners and virtual maps while Kira and Mason rested in the nearby spacecraft.

Now it was daytime, and all Sarah could think about was the quill she'd extracted from Mason's leg. Every planet had its malevolents, and every malevolent had its adaptation. On Earth, it was shapeshifting. On Samoia, it was quills infused with poison that could function independently of their host. Aroyan malevolents were as radioactive as their surroundings, and other malevolents elsewhere had learned to magnify previously dormant or unimpressive abilities. Without proper training, defending oneself against an attack—especially a coordinated group effort—was next to impossible.

"Galloway."

Both mother and daughter turned to see Damien walking toward them.

"I'll assume you were addressing me," Sarah said as the sand gave way to grass, which blanketed the hillside in swaths of green.

Flicking his eyes at Kira, Damien gave a half-nod in Sarah's direction and lowered his voice. "I think there's something you need to see."

Sarah touched her daughter's hand, stealing her attention away from a clump of flowers. "Why don't you see if Mason's feeling better? Get him to walk, if you can."

Kira glanced between her mother and the man on the ridge, then nodded and headed back to the Commander.

Once she was out of earshot, Damien said, "We have company."

"Malevolents?"

"I'm not sure."

Sarah cocked her brow. "What else could they be?"

"Humans?"

"There are no humans on Samoia."

"Are you sure about that?"

Sarah clenched her jaw. A lifetime wouldn't be long enough to learn the ways of this enigmatic planet—a planet that had never seemed suitable for human habitation; a rogue sphere the size of Mercury with a similar, quicksilver nature. Centuries ago, Ansel had toyed with the idea of introducing a nomadic tribe, but feared that chasing the illusions would lead humans into a life of eternal dissatisfaction. Turns out, they did this everywhere, but nowhere was it more obvious than on planet Earth.

They walked slowly, trying not to trip over the rocks sequestered in the dense undergrowth. Sarah glimpsed her Keepsake to find the stone bleeding red—a sure sign that evil was near, even if the current topography was as serene as a postcard.

"They're close," Damien said from up ahead.

"I know." Sarah surveyed the hillside. The farther they walked, the taller the grass became until she could no longer see the Commander or her partner. Even the sound of his footsteps failed to cut through the wall of vegetation.

She rolled forward onto her toes in order to peer above the waves. "Damien?"

The grass rustled softly in the breeze. Sarah consulted her ring again: a deep, roiling crimson streaked with silver, which indicated the presence of a benevolent being. The two colours separated briefly, then collided in sudden confrontation that turned the entire Keepsake—even the band—flaming orange.

She yanked the fiery circle off her finger. The Keepsake arced through the air and summersaulted to a stop in the loamy soil as the quarreling hues faded to black. Sarah stared at the salmon-pink blister encircling her finger. Red and silver was the rarest of pairings: The last time she'd seen it was the day The Establishment collapsed. Even then, nothing had burned or bubbled or blistered. Everything had simply... disappeared.

Sarah shot to her feet, snatched up the handful of dirt containing her corrupted Keepsake, and dashed through the grass maze, hoping she was running toward the Commander instead of away from it. Toward her daughter. Toward everything.

Blind and frantic, she glided through the emerald ribbons like scissors. But sometimes, even the sharpest blades got stuck—hit a snag that stopped them mid-shear. Sarah didn't feel the snag so much as she saw her path to Kira suddenly break. The blue sky crumpled as she plunged to the ground. Her Keepsake flipped out of her hand and landed a few feet away, mocking her with its unblinking eye. She slid it back onto her finger for safekeeping, then flipped herself over to see what she'd tripped on.

An orange uniform, stained black in the centre, with a hole so deep that grass had started to fill it—right where Damien's essence used to be.

Sarah scrambled toward her partner, whose eyes were trapped open inside his skull. His skin was ice-cold, his field nonexistent. Even his Keepsake had turned white—a blank page that no longer told the story of his life.

She held his head in her hands. Grief was not something she was accustomed to feeling; in her line of work, it could even be considered a hinderance. But Damien had been more than a colleague to her: he'd been a loyal friend, a tireless listener, and the closest thing Kira had to a father. He'd made her existence at The Establishment feel normal—another illusion, shattered.

Sarah closed her eyes and pressed her lips against his brow. Then, she gently laid his head down and folded his hands on his chest. Without his essence, she couldn't send his vessel back to Ansel for disposal. All she could do was let him go.

"In another life, I'll find a way to thank you," she whispered.

Suddenly, the grass receded. The tall stalks shrunk to thorny clusters of cacti and stinging nettle. Sarah leapt to her feet as a burst of Yucca emerged from the sandy basin, nearly impaling her on its spear-like leaves.

Out here, it wasn't the only thing that wanted to destroy her.

She spun a tight circle, taking inventory of her surroundings. Against the powder blue sky, the rusty knuckles of rock shone as brightly as forged iron, giving off a heat that threatened to strangle her. There weren't many creatures that thrived in these conditions, and the ones that did were typically cold-blooded.

Malevolents did everything in cold blood.

Sarah turned back to the horizon and froze, eyeing the figure standing amidst the trees.

"Good evening, Sarah," the black-eyed being said, tall and unmoving, like he was trying to pass for the saguaro's shadow.

"It's not dark yet," she returned, keeping her tone steady.

"It will be soon." The creature chuckled, inclining his head toward the setting sun. "This is Samoia after all."

Silhouettes danced on the fringes of her vision. A sharp racket echoed in her skull as the shadows closed in and knocked her unconscious.

Darker Than Black

"They've been gone a really long time," Kira fretted, completing her fourth lap around the room. "Do you think we should go and look for them?"

She glanced toward the vertical tube encasing Mason's form. Three of the recharging pods had been targeted by projectiles in the crash; a fourth had been shorn off its support rods by an intrepid metal beam. Damien had managed—with Mason's vocabulary—to reconnect the remaining cylinders, but it wouldn't be long before the Commander's backup generators failed and the pods lost power. Hopefully, Mason's leg would be healed by then. Kira wasn't as optimistic about her shoulder, or the crater in her side that made the entire right half of her vessel feel as if it belonged to someone else.

"I'm sure they're fine," he said in a tinny voice. "Probably went for another walk."

"A long one." Kira stopped pacing and took a seat on the edge of the beam. "You don't think—"

"They're Hunters, like us. I'm sure they've already set up a quarantine zone for the malevolents and are well on their way to locating the crew." Confined to the bullet-shaped sarcophagus until every last particle of energy had been assigned to its proper position, Mason found himself becoming restless with boredom. He shifted his weight to test the strength in his injured leg and asked, "What colour's your Keepsake?"

Kira consulted her ring. "Silver and…" She squinted at the oculus. "That's weird. It's… turning white."

Mason opened the door and poked his head into the annular room, his face sporting a similar hue. After a brief pause, he stepped out of the glowing column and crossed the room to kneel in front of his partner.

"See?" Kira extended her left hand. "It's silver in the middle because you're here, but around the edges it's white."

He nodded and draped his fingers over hers. As he lifted his gaze, he couldn't help but notice the unnatural way in which she held her arm. Her shoulder bulged under the red material. Moving slowly, he raised his hand to the swollen joint, causing her to wince.

"Does that hurt?" he asked.

"It's not that bad," Kira replied, focusing on her Keepsake once more. "So, I was thinking we should search for the crew first, since they've been here the longest. After that—"

"*We* are not going anywhere. There's enough power in the recharging pod to put a temporary patch on your shoulder, but it won't survive the stress of a full-scale search and rescue mission." Mason stood up. "I'll go. By myself. And if I run into your mother along the way, I'll send her straight here to doctor you."

Kira scowled. "As I was saying: the crew needs us. If we can get to higher ground, we might be able to start a signal fire. As long as we keep it burning, our friends will be able to find us."

"Assuming the malevolents don't find us first. Then what? You're going to dredge up a bunch of corrupted memories and build an orb big enough for everyone to shelter under? Your Keepsake is dying. You couldn't defend yourself against *one* malevolent, much less a whole pack if the circumstances called for it."

"Don't tell me what I can do!" She shot to her feet, thankful for the beam's head start. "I am Sarah and Gabe's daughter. My parents sacrificed everything so that people like you wouldn't end up floating around in a vacuum. If I fade into oblivion before the mission is over, then so be it, because I will know that I did everything I could to bring our comrades home."

A smile spread across Mason's face. "You're right: I shouldn't tell you what to do." He waited until Kira had stopped swaying before releasing her arm. "Lead the way, soldier."

Once they reached the exit, Kira pressed the button to lower the ramp. The hinges grated in protest, but the barrier remained firmly sealed.

A ring of stark, grey light haloed the room. The cockpit sat directly above, at the top of a steep flight of stairs adorned with blue jewels to make nighttime navigation less hazardous. Insufficient power seemed like an unlikely explanation for the ramp's inertia.

Mason appeared at Kira's side. "What's wrong?"

"I don't know. The door's stuck or something." Kira tried the button again. This time, the rectangular portal popped free of its frame, allowing a sliver of sunlight to penetrate the dust-laden air.

He flattened his hands against the rubberized surface and pushed, to no avail. It was a sunny day outside, but that didn't deter the dark cloud of dread looming over their inoperable spacecraft.

"It's not an issue with the power," Mason said. "I think something's blocking the ramp."

He turned and took the stairs two at a time. The cockpit would provide a three-hundred-and-sixty-degree view of the problem, as well as any threats that may be lurking on the fringes. Kira peered through the crack at the clear sky beyond, then glanced at her Keepsake to find the foreboding hue spreading like frost across the watery black eye.

"I was right: we're basically in the middle of a giant rock garden, with a boulder directly outside the door," he called down to her.

"Can't you move it, somehow?"

"If it was just one boulder, I'd try, but there's nowhere for it to go." He descended the stairs, shaking his head with each step. "Looks like we're going to have to wait it out. Hopefully Samoia's next act won't involve a flash flood." Once he reached the floor, he brushed his hands together and looked around at the dim shapes and long, quivering shadows. "Well, Miss Galloway. Got any ideas?"

"Yes."

"I'm all ears."

She furrowed her brows. "What?"

Mason pretended to sigh. "It means 'I'm listening.'"

Kira motioned to one of the hallways. A relentless clanging could be heard coming from the floor below it, followed by a series of whispers that sounded like an approaching thunderstorm. The hairs on Mason's arms bristled in response to the electricity sizzling around them.

"There's another door down in the cargo hold," she explained. "I'm sure the rocks will have moved by the time we reach it."

"You mean the unloading bay," Mason said, looking uncertain. He waved his hand at the piles of misplaced equipment littering the cabin and added, "You don't think it would be safer to wait it out here? After all, we don't know how many malevolents the crew was transporting, or if any of them escaped during the crash."

"If you're going to argue with everything I say, then don't bother asking for my input."

"I'm not arguing. I'm voicing a reasonable concern."

"So, instead of taking a calculated risk for the crew, my mother, and Damien, you'd rather sit here and wait for an unknowable amount of time until the rocks either move under their own will or we drown?"

"I wouldn't put it quite like that." Mason scratched his head, making his hair stand on end. "Fine. If you think it's safe, then we'll cut through the cargo hold. But don't expect me to save you if a malevolent tries to make you its next meal." He intended for this last part to be a joke, and hoped Kira wouldn't take it too seriously.

She lifted her good shoulder and smirked. "That's okay. I probably wouldn't satisfy them in my state anyway." She patted his arm, emphasizing the abundance of energy cushioning his vessel, and disappeared into the belly of the spacecraft.

The lower deck was at war with itself: steam gunned through the pipes while sparks gushed from exposed wires, making the walls look like they were bleeding fire. Despite his initial reluctance, Mason insisted on leading the way. He treaded cautiously over the metallic minefield, dodging fallen screws and puddles of unknown origin, and paused occasionally to listen for anything out of the ordinary. Kira's mind rumbled with worry over her mother and Damien, making it difficult to hear anything in the disheveled labyrinth.

The door to the containment area was still sealed. Mason raised his hand to the metal barrier. An opaque circle formed around his fingers as dozens of pale blue tanks faded into view, offering a glimpse into the room on the other side. Given the state of the surrounding spacecraft, Kira had expected to see broken glass and hungry malevolents circling the flooded room like sharks. The emergency exit was located at the other end of the holding bay, past the giant spools of pale blue water and seething red eyes.

Mason moved his hand away. "Looks safe to me."

"What had Jonathon said at The Establishment?" Kira asked rhetorically. "'A certain amount of damage is inevitable.'"

"You're not still upset about that comment, are you?"

"No. I'm just saying he might be useful for something after all." She walked over to the scanner and applied her left hand to the keypad. A flash of green illuminated her face as the heavy metal door glided open.

She entered the room first and stared up at the cylindrical fixtures. Each one was twenty feet tall and ten feet in diameter, with a ladder fastened to the external wall like an enormous zipper. A regular infusion of calming serum, delivered via a network of spigots gridding the ceiling, thwarted the inhabitants' escape. Kira wondered how long it had been since the last dose was administered—and how long it would take the malevolents to realize there was no one guarding the doors.

Mason studied his Keepsake. The stone had turned an alarming shade of red, but there was no sign of a breach anywhere. He lifted his gaze to Kira, who was standing next to one of the enclosures, observing the restless black shape in silence.

"You don't trust me," she said. It took Mason a moment to realize she was talking to him.

He approached her slowly. The malevolent's serpentine body coiled apoplectically as it bared its wall of deadly yellow teeth.

"I can feel your energy," Kira went on, "you're afraid I'm going to turn on you—join the enemy." She gestured to their specimen.

"I'm not afraid of you. I just don't think it's a good idea to linger."

Panning his eyes over the room, Mason sensed a shift in the inmates' behaviour. A stream of bubbles juddered to the surface of the adjacent pool as the monster within emerged from the deep, its long, tattered tail matching the width of Mason's chest. One by one, the other malevolents rose from their watery graves, grinning and hungry for revenge.

"Kira—"

"I'm not dangerous," she insisted, turning back to him. "No matter what Dean thinks, I have no intention of possessing anyone, Living or otherwise."

"That's very reassuring, but right now I think we should focus on getting out of here before—"

Mason glanced down at the floor. A puddle of murky black water rippled past his boots. It crept steadily in Kira's direction until she raised her eyes to its source.

Freed from the confines of its aqueous prison, the malevolent had taken on the appearance of a severely malnourished wolf. It navigated the floor on stilt-like limbs, its ribs poking through the skin like blunt daggers. Two glowing, scarlet eyes narrowed on the intruders, and a chilling growl poured from its fiery pink throat.

Water splashed onto the floor at Kira's feet. The Commander was losing power—and with it, the ability to control its cargo. Rather than a powerful surge of neon-blue sedative, the spigots merely sputtered. A haze of bubbles blotted the cantankerous creatures from view as they thrashed against the walls, cracking the glass.

"Kira," Mason said in a low voice. "Go."

"What about you?"

"It's okay. I'll hold them back so you can get to the exit. Once you're outside, get to high ground as quickly as possible."

"I'm not leaving without you. We came to Samoia together. We—"

He held up his hand as she fell silent. "We had a good run, and I'd do it again in a heartbeat." Mason glimpsed the glistering blue orb suspended between his fingers. The longer they stayed here, the more the malevolents fed on their fear. The monsters grew, casting a thick, black smoke over the holding bay.

Mason smiled at her. "See you on the other side."

The orb disintegrated in a blinding white flash. Broken glass sprayed through the air as Kira sprinted toward the door. The lights along the wall flickered as several malevolents succumbed to Mason's orb, dissolving into the electrified flood with a hellish screech. The orb would protect him temporarily, but as his memories faded, so would the walls around him.

Kira applied her hand to the scanner and looked back over her shoulder. Between the crashing waves and the toppling towers, she couldn't see Mason at all. Couldn't hear him. Couldn't sense him. The emergency exit opened, and with one final glance at the boiling water, she ran through the door and toward the nearest peak.

The Commander hemorrhaged monsters. Soon the landscape was teeming with maggoty black shapes, all of them writhing in the carcass of a dried riverbed. Kira scaled the rocky hillside until pain and grief shackled her feet to the ground. She sat down on the crumbling soil and gazed helplessly at the remains of their shelter, now an inhospitable shell of useless technology and unsolved mysteries. She still didn't see Mason anywhere.

Kira turned her attention to the wound in her side. Tarry energy oozed through the bandage, making her right arm feel heavier than her left. The surrounding stones and shrubs turned pink as destabilization sickness set in, altering her perception of reality. The longer she went without treatment, the more she struggled to distinguish injury from illusion: the sky had shifted to chartreuse, and the valley cradling the Commander's circular bulk shimmered like a hot sidewalk, heralding its imminent transformation. She looked for Mason amidst the detritus of the purged spacecraft, but by the time she identified the red uniform, it had already disappeared.

She didn't move. Short green spikes pushed through the dirt at her feet until the whole ground was covered in a thick carpet of grass. Wildflowers bloomed around her, indifferent to the massacre that had preceded them. Kira felt insulted by their colours—so bright and cheerful that her grief felt darker than black, deeper than bottomless, and longer than forever. She had escaped certain death only to find herself craving its embrace, yearning to be with the man she'd left behind.

"Damn you," she muttered, unsure if she was talking to the planet, the malevolents, or herself. Fire filled her eyes as she lifted her gaze to the sun, daring it to match her fury.

After some time, Kira composed herself, stood up, and started walking toward the mountains in the distance. There was nothing left of the spacecraft—only a wide groove in Samoia's crust that now belonged to a swarm of birds pecking the eyes out of a particularly unlucky malevolent.

She'd barely taken ten steps when she heard her name. It was faint. She stopped and looked around. From her elevated vantage point, she could see the sky changing colours in the distance, going from blue to copper in a matter of moments. The wind strengthened, bending the trees until she thought the roots might burst through the soil. Even the birds, feasting blissfully on a smorgasbord of shapeshifters stranded in the mud, took to the skies in a chorus of terror. Kira heard her name again and turned back to face the valley.

As she did, an indistinct red shape came into view. She checked her Keepsake, just in case. Sure enough, the stone—which never lied—was pure silver.

"Mason," she whispered. Then she screamed it. "Mason!"

He staggered on the uneven terrain. Barely able to hold his head up, much less climb a thirty-degree incline, he collapsed in the dirt and let the waves of pink and green wash over him at last. Kira skidded on the loose rocks and slid down to where he had fallen, wrapping her arms around his shoulders.

"The Commander is gone," he croaked.

"I know." She sat back and studied his face. Water dripped from his hair, and dull grey scratches latticed his face. His eyes were hollow, haunted by the horrors he'd endured. But he was here, and that was all that mattered. "How did you get out?"

"The same way you did: through the door. All that water gave me a nice little push."

"I saw—I mean, I *thought* I saw you floating down the river." She picked up his left hand to transfer some of her energy into his Keepsake. "I thought the malevolents had destroyed you."

"They nearly did. I used the longest memory chain I had, but I couldn't recall everything with equal clarity, so my orb started to crack. Eventually, the weight of the water caused the entire structure to collapse. I got swept away." Mason pointed to the trees scattered along the riverbed. "I grabbed hold of the first solid object I saw. The river was moving too fast for the malevolents to do the same."

They sat in silence on the hillside, watching the last of the water drain into the canyon.

Mason turned his focus to the sky. He'd never seen clouds so dense on planet Earth; they seemed even more ominous here, especially when the first drop of water solidified into a hard, white sphere. It ricocheted off the ground and struck his knee with a painful pop.

"Hail?" Kira said as he picked up the pea-sized projectile.

Mason rolled it in his hand and shook his head. "Not hail," he replied, chancing another look at the sky, "rocks."

She leapt to her feet. "That's not possible."

"Ever heard the phrase 'the sky is falling'?"

Another pebble, this one slightly larger than the first, plummeted toward its target. It missed Kira's face by mere inches.

"I have now," she barked.

As the storm intensified, the stones swelled to the size of boulders. The ground quaked under the assault of an aerial army, and a thunderclap split the mountain like a peanut shell. Craters gouged the planet's surface as Kira and Mason raced for the cover of a cave. No sooner had they vanished into the pitch-black cleft than the floor crumbled beneath their feet, plunging them into the turquoise lake below.

Uncharted

Sarah awoke in a strange room. She peered up at the concrete walls before placing her hand against the cold surface of her prison, her mind churning for an explanation. Samoia had never been populated by humans, yet the room's architecture seemed to suggest some kind of mechanical intervention. On the far side of the cell was a steel door—possibly an illusion, as most forms of freedom tended to be. Sarah studied the smoky grey rectangle, expecting her only hope of escape to suddenly disappear.

The door didn't move. She climbed to her feet, but only managed to take two steps before reaching the end of her tether. The chain rattled mockingly as she jerked her arm again, to no avail. Sarah crouched in the corner and summoned a light to inspect her restraints. Both the chain and the cuff it led to were in mint condition. Worse, the band encircling her wrist appeared to have no hinges or seams she could pry. The entire contraption was unbreakably solid, and far more complex than anything the human mind could engineer. She gave the metal links another decisive yank, then sank down on the floor and closed her eyes, picturing Kira.

In the dark, time didn't exist. Every once in a while, Sarah would run her hand along the interlocking loops, feeling for weak spots she could manipulate. Using her light consumed too much energy. She tried not to think too much either, knowing that isolation was a shortcut to insanity. Not that she was in a mood to reminisce: the last thing she remembered was finding Damien's empty vessel and cradling his head in her lap. Now she was trapped here—alone—with no way to contact The Establishment and no way of knowing if Kira was okay. What kind of mother did that make her?

Before she could answer her own question, the door swung open and a dark figure walked in, silhouetted by the bright light of the hallway behind him.

Sarah squinted at the object in his hand. A chair. Where had he gotten a chair from?

"I see you exist comfortably down here," she said.

"Quite," he agreed, setting the chair in the middle of the room and taking a seat. "I'm beginning to sense you're not enjoying your stay though."

"Where I come from, we don't usually chain our guests to the walls." She indicated the shackle. "I have to admit, I'm perplexed by this mechanism. Normally I'd be able to bust myself out, but… no dice."

"Now, that's no way to behave in someone's home, Miss Galloway. You should be ashamed."

"I know what you're trying to do, and it's not working."

Her host leaned forward. His coal-black eyes glinted insouciantly as he cocked his head. His rotted teeth flashed in a perverted grin.

"Oh, do you? Then why are you cowering in the corner like a little mouse? I thought you were immune to my influence."

"Your influence, yes. But not your stench."

The malevolent's laughter rang through the room with deafening delight. Sarah flinched as he rose and took a step toward her, kneeling on one knee to get a better look at her face.

"The Cadillac of insults," he said. "And before you ask: yes, I know all about that lovely daughter of yours and what makes her so dangerous. You may think you hate me, but deep down, you know we want the same thing. You and I are more alike than you realize, Sarah."

A chill swept through her as Gabe's memory rose to the surface of her Keepsake. She kept a straight face, suppressing all traces of emotion. This was a test: just like she'd been looking for a way out, her captor was searching for a way into her mind.

"Kira isn't dangerous," Sarah said. "Just because she's—"

"A malevolent. The very thing you've been trained to destroy. That's why you permitted her to come here, isn't it? Part of you was hoping she wouldn't return, and that you'd finally be free to move up the ladder and take Ansel's job."

"That's not true. I chose to stay at The Establishment long before I was aware of her existence."

"But she is trouble," the malevolent stated, catching Sarah's interest. "More than you're capable of handling. Motherhood versus career. A timeless dilemma."

"The only dilemma I have to make is whether I should destroy you now or wait for backup. The longer you talk about my daughter, the closer I get to making a decision." The chain echoed her steely threat.

Her adversary towered over her. The smile had vanished from his face, and in its place, Sarah saw only teeth: deadly yellow daggers cutting through his manufactured charm.

"Where's my daughter?" Sarah demanded as he picked up the chair and walked toward the door, where two of his subordinates waited.

"I wish I knew. Until then, you may want to work on your escape plan."

She leapt to her feet. The chain stiffened behind her as he reached for the door and grinned demonically. "Sleep well, your highness."

●

Kira didn't know how long she'd been underwater. She tumbled in the greenish fog, tethered to an invisible puppet master by long strings of bubbles on her hands and feet. Her movements were slow and cumbersome and her visibility was poor. The light was everywhere, yet it appeared to have no distinct source. It certainly couldn't have come from the sun, since—as far as she knew—they were in a cave, seeking shelter from a deadly downpour of rocks. The water stretched for miles, dizzyingly vast and unsettlingly empty, like a bluer, colder version of the in-between, the existential void on which The Establishment had been built. Centring her field, Kira lifted both arms above her head and kicked off her chains as she rose.

She surfaced from the deep and looked around. Steep, crystallized walls curved above her head to form a shimmering white dome. A pinprick of light in the ceiling indicated where they'd fallen through. Surely, such a delicate beam couldn't illuminate a hidden sea, she reasoned. But this was Samoia, and anything was possible.

She swam toward the edge of the water, hoping that the jagged crystals climbing the walls meant there was land nearby. With any luck, Mason wouldn't be far behind.

Kira reached for a cluster of pink quartz shaped like a lily; the formation shattered under her touch. When she tried to reach for its neighbour, it, too, crumbled to a fine powder. Kira fell backwards with a gasp. As she sank beneath the surface again, she thought she heard a voice calling her name. Her hand fell away from her side, and a cloud of inky blood dissipated into the surrounding water.

A crimson blur swam toward her. Kira closed her eyes, surrendering to her battle with the blackness as the mysterious object reached for her arm. Up she floated, her hair spinning like a slow-motion tornado around her face.

Mason burst through the surface with Kira slumped in his arms. He rowed toward a narrow patch of sand, then climbed to his feet, lifted both of her arms, and dragged her out of the water.

Kira's eyelids flickered. A short distance away, she could vaguely discern the shape of a doorway and the shadow of a tunnel beyond it. Mason crouched beside her, shaking his head as he inspected the wound.

"You're losing a lot of energy," he said. His facial features were still blurry, but she heard the concern in his voice as clear as day. "Can you hear me, Kira?"

"Yes."

"Okay. Just hang in there. I'm going to redress the wound and boost your Keepsake, then we'll see what's on the other end of that tunnel."

Blobs of colour danced before Kira's eyes. Crystals sprouted from the ceiling in patches of blue, violet, frost, and fuchsia, but she was mesmerized by a beauty of a different kind. Out of the corner of her eye, she saw the bony ridge of Mason's spine, the pale hills of his shoulders, and the broad plain of his undressed back, hunched over the white undershirt he'd removed and was now tearing into strips of equal width. Once the cloth bandages had been prepared, he reached for his red shirt and slipped his arms back into the sleeves. He buttoned the uniform closed, then scooped up his materials and turned to face her.

"Can you sit up?" he asked.

She raised herself onto her elbows. Lifting the hem of her shirt, she watched as Mason used one of the shreds to mop up the inky residue with gentle motions. Looking at him now, it seemed impossible to believe that he'd willingly injected himself with poison in a previous life. She tried to imagine the bruises on his arms, the sunken cheeks, and the permanent state of misery that had driven him to desperation and, eventually, death.

"Why did you do it?" she asked as he folded a strip and stuck it to the wound. "All the drugs."

Mason concentrated on his work. Wrapping a length of fabric around her torso, he said, "I was messed up, Kira. Sometimes I think it was better for the people who knew me that my life ended when it did."

"At least you're not half-malevolent," she replied, flinching at the pressure in her ribs.

"That's true... but my addiction did possess me. It took over my whole life. At first it was just one hit at a party, then, before I knew it, I'd lost my job, my apartment, my girlfriend. All I thought about was my next fix. I went down a long, dark road with no map, and once I realized I was lost, there was no going home."

"What do you think you'll do after you regenerate?"

He shrugged, smiling as he added another layer of the stretchy material. "I don't know yet. I thought I might like to be a doctor."

"My mom wanted to be a doctor when she was alive."

"What about you? I doubt you'll be at The Establishment forever."

Kira looked at him, then down at his hands. "I don't know. Maybe I'll be a pilot, or a soldier."

Mason tied a knot in the cloth and sat back to admire his handiwork. "How does that feel?"

"Good as new."

"Great." He held out his left hand for her to take. "Now your Keepsake."

Once the transfer of energy was complete, Mason helped Kira to stand up before turning his attention over to the tunnel. By now, he was accustomed to finding passageways in odd places: during his time at The Establishment, he'd escorted thousands of spirits through otherwise solid barriers, like brick walls and locked doors. But he'd never seen a portal like this before, no matter how much experience he had with tunnel vision.

Mason rested a hand on one of the pillars. It looked and felt solid—and so did the darkness staring back at him.

"These supports are made of timber," he stated matter-of-factly. Kira observed his explorations without comment, trying to grasp the significance of them. "It's an old mine shaft. See the beams?"

"What would a mine be doing on Samoia?"

"I don't know. It couldn't be manmade, and yet…" Mason took several steps forward. It wasn't long before he became invisible.

A pale blue light sparked in the distance. It lasted only a few seconds before flickering out.

"Mason?" Kira called, tensing at the echo that followed his name.

"I'm okay," he said. "Just a little low on energy."

"Can you see an exit?"

"Not yet. But we should keep moving. Can you walk?"

"I think so." She laid a hand on her newly dressed wound. She wasn't yet used to the tightness of the new binding, but the pressure kept her motivated, like a poke in the ribs from a supportive friend.

She took a step forward and disappeared into the shadows.

They walked in silence down the long hallway, guided by the waning glow of Mason's light. The tunnel had low ceilings and dirt floors, and it went on indefinitely, with no obvious destination or purpose. Kira felt suffocated by its dullness. It didn't seem like it belonged in the same cave where she'd encountered a crystal garden and sparkling blue waters. Another trick of the eye, perhaps—or the calm before the storm.

Eventually, Mason stopped and scooped up a handful of dirt. It rolled off his palm in a powdery white mist, confirming his suspicions.

"What's wrong?" Kira asked.

Mason dug his hand into the dirt again. Holding his fist a few inches above his boots, he watched the sand stream from his fingers and curve slightly before touching the ground.

"There's a breeze," he said quietly. He raised his eyes to hers. "Normally, the air in a tunnel is dead. Nothing comes in, nothing goes out. But it seems like the sand is moving, which means—"

"The tunnel is moving."

Mason rose and aimed his light in a circular motion, hunting for evidence of Kira's claim. The beams showed no signs of bowing and the ground didn't quake under their feet. If it was so easy to imagine chaos, why couldn't he envision peace?

"Maybe," he said, lowering his hand. "Let's keep moving. There has to be a way out of here."

Kira summoned her own light. It wasn't much—her fingers were barely visible—but the act of funneling her precious energy into a single task stole her attention away from worrying that they may never see daylight again. She'd volunteered to come here, and she felt partially responsible for whatever happened next. She shone her light straight ahead, but saw only dirt walls, wooden beams, and an impenetrable black void staring back at them like a cyclopean eye.

Mason cleared his throat. "Kira?"

"Yes?"

"I was going to wait until after we got back to The Establishment to tell you this, but—" He paused and waited for her to turn around. As she did, a smile formed on his face. "I've decided to delay my regeneration. So, I guess we'll be seeing a lot more of each other from now on."

"Oh," Kira said after some pause. She waved her hand at the distance they'd already covered and asked, "But what about all that stuff you said about wanting to become a doctor?"

"It's just… what if I get a fresh start and I screw it up? I don't know if I can trust myself to make the right choices the next time around, especially if Ansel wipes my memories."

"He wipes out memories of The Establishment for a reason. But every baby is born with a few seed memories, right? Ansel picks the ones that define us the most, and it's up to us to follow the proper path."

"And what if the 'proper path' looks like this?" Mason gestured to their surroundings. "Maybe it's better not to risk it. I'll stick with what I already know—for eternity, if that's what it takes."

Kira smiled to hide her disappointment. For a moment, she'd nearly fooled herself into believing he was staying because of her. "Maybe you should talk to Ansel first."

As he opened his mouth to respond, a glimmer of movement caught Kira's eyes. She directed her light at the overhead beams just as a small stone plummeted to the floor, dislodged by the shifting dirt.

Another rock fell and bounced off the ground with a dull plink. Mason and Kira stared at each other.

"Run," he said.

She hurled herself into the blackness. The timber trusses groaned as the walls closed in, bending the wooden bones until they broke.

One by one, the beams split in two. Each explosion produced a lethal cloud of wood shards accompanied by a terrific bang. Kira felt the floor shake under her feet. One misstep, and they'd be trapped here forever, like leaves pressed between the pages of an ancient book.

Then she saw a door. The wall surrounding it was made of bright red bricks—and seeing red was never a good sign, especially on Samoia.

She grabbed the handle and twisted, but the door didn't budge. She threw her shoulder against the metal barrier and growled in pain, but still nothing happened. The ceiling continued to buckle, churning up a gigantic cloud of dust as the tunnel closed like a fist.

"Open it," Mason ordered.

"I'm trying." Kira pushed harder, ignoring the pain in her side. Blackness clawed at the edges of her vision.

Stepping around her, Mason jiggled the knob while applying force with his shoulder. Finally, on the third beat, the door gave way, swinging inward to reveal a small, dark room with concrete walls. They slipped inside, then leaned against the door as the last of the rubble filled the empty space, and the tunnel fell silent at last.

He lifted his head to look at her. "Are you okay?"

"I don't know." Kira took several steps back from the door. Slipping a hand under her right arm, she prodded the sore spot between her ribs. The dressing was still dry, but if she wanted to get better, she had to get back to The Establishment.

Mason walked to the centre of the mysterious room and stared up at the smooth grey walls, pondering the purpose of so much wasted space. He only saw one door, and it was clear they wouldn't be passing through it again.

"I'm sorry for bringing you here," Kira whispered, bending forward and placing her hands on her knees. "I thought I could be a hero, but I've just made everything worse."

"I'm the one who disobeyed the orders. It wasn't a rescue mission—and now we're the ones who need to be saved."

"I doubt anyone knows we're here, wherever *here* is…"

"The Devil's Throat," came a low voice from the shadows. A figure manifested from the dark triangle where the walls met the floor. A dirty white pinion trailed behind it like a king's robes, still majestic despite its obvious neglect.

"The only ones who know your exact location are the malevolents, and their intentions are far from heroic," the being said, looking at each of his visitors. His sky-blue eyes shone brightly against his dark brown skin. "No one is looking for you. And if they are, Samoia will ensure you are never found."

Mason turned to Kira with wide eyes. He lowered his voice and said, "I've been dead too long. I don't even know what's real anymore, and what isn't."

"Me neither," she replied, "and I've never set foot on Earth."

"Are you finished?" the prisoner asked, his brows creasing at the interruption.

"Not quite," Kira replied. She sized up the monster in their midst: a plainclothes giant nearly seven feet tall with one white wing folded neatly against his back and the other drooping powerlessly toward the floor. "What are you, exactly?"

"Isn't it obvious?" The being's annoyance deepened. "I'm one of Ansel's Elite. An Angel."

"That's—"

"Impossible, Mr. Massey? Tell me: of all the wonders you've witnessed since arriving on Samoia, why would my existence baffle you more than a hailstorm of rocks or a lake with no bottom?"

"I'm alarmed at how much you already know," Mason admitted.

"Your ignorance is equally shocking," the Angel replied.

"There must be more creatures like you," Kira interjected. "Right?"

As the Angel approached, he cast a shadow over her that was both frightening and exhilarating. Dwarfed by the presence of a spiritually superior entity, she wondered if this was how humans felt in the moments before death: supplicant and chagrined, waiting to be taken higher than they'd ever gone before.

"There were," he explained. "You have your mother's sight, yes?"

"What's he talking about?" Mason asked.

"It was part of her immunity," Kira explained. "After she became Earth-bound, she could see the energy around her, even in inanimate objects. I have the same ability, and because I'm… a malevolent… I can see what's going to happen, in addition to what already has. When we were cleaning the tanks, I saw Dean being condemned, and I panicked because I thought… I thought maybe Ansel would send me there, too."

"It's a rare gift," the Angel added, capturing Mason's gaze. "A useful one, too. Kira will be able to see all the passageways, once she's airborne."

"Am I the only one still making sense around here?" Mason asked, getting no answer.

The winged overseer ignored him. "Go ahead, Kira."

She looked up. High above her head, an image formed, rising out of the darkness like steam from a tea kettle. She heard screams, voices trapped in the walls from the souls that had been taken here. Six winged fighters, dressed in ivory and gold, ascended toward the ceiling, disguised as a luminous blue sphere. She heard the first flyer collide with the rock and the crackling of his bones in the confusion of feathers that floated back down. One by one, until they were all gone, until the air was thick with down and the scent of spilled blood. Until only one remained.

"An entire race, gone in the blink of an eye," the Angel stated somberly as Kira's vision cleared.

"Except you," Mason said.

"Under the present circumstances, I'd hardly consider myself to be a proper representation of my specie."

"And Ansel hasn't tried to contact you?" Kira ventured.

"Not to my knowledge. In either case, a million years is a long time to hold a grudge."

"So what happened to your wing?" Mason asked.

The Angel tore his attention from Kira and gave her partner a once-over. "Training accident," he answered, making it clear he didn't intend to elaborate.

"We crashed. We were looking for the crew of—"

"Commander 3. I know."

Kira's eyes widened. "Do you know where they are?"

The being circled them, his once strong and powerful limb dragging along the cold foundation. The feathers near the floor had become thin and frayed like the ends of an old rope, tying their owner to his fate. "Yes. But knowing where something is, is not the same as knowing how to get to it."

"But you're an Angel," Mason argued. "Can't you just—"

"Fly out of here?" The orotund voice dripped with contempt. "Unlike you, I've learned from my mistakes." The creature continued, unruffled by Mason's incinerating glare. "The only way you're going to reach your friends is through flight. Unfortunately, your rings' navigation systems won't work on Samoia, and certainly not in the lair. Not unless you're one of them."

"So, help me understand this," Mason said. "Only malevolents can see the path, but only Angels can follow it?"

"What about my mother?" Kira interjected. "Have you seen her? Do you know where she is?"

"She's here. No word on her health."

"I'm not sure where you're getting your information, but I'm sure Sarah is fine," Mason said, mainly for Kira's benefit. "It's the crew we're concerned about. They've gone too long without a connection to The Establishment. Which begs the question: how are you still standing?"

The Angel smirked. "With difficulty." Turning to Kira again, he offered his left hand, his Keepsake glowing gold in the dusky chamber. "Take it."

Kira glanced over at Mason, who nodded. Then she slipped her fingers into the Angel's grasp and squeezed.

A burst of light emanated from Kira's Keepsake, set ablaze by the spark of power that ran through her at the Angel's touch. A searing pain curled along her spine and into her shoulders. Kira sank to her knees, terminating the connection as the vortex of memories dissipated into the chilly air.

She hunched over her lap, pinned in place by an inexplicable weight on her back. A single, damp raven feather plunged to the floor next to her Keepsake, which flaunted a sky-blue stone.

The Angel cupped her chin in his hand. "Fly."

She turned her head reluctantly. Sure enough, the feather had not been an illusion. Her back was covered in thousands of glossy black vanes, each one attached to a pair of bony parentheses.

Kira stood up. A twenty-foot shadow accompanied her.

"Fly," the Angel ordered again.

She rolled her shoulders, getting a feel for the mechanics of her retrofitted extremities. The joints opened like well-oiled hinges, allowing her to see for the first time the size and shape of the Angel's gift. Kira stared at her silhouette on the wall, then gave an experimental flap that whipped her hair around her face.

She bent her knees slightly, then beat her wings in a powerful gust that nearly knocked Mason off his feet. She lifted off the floor, then tumbled in mid-air before landing on her front.

The Angel reached out, catching Mason by the arm. "Don't help her. She won't learn if she doesn't struggle."

"She's injured."

"She was." Mason arched his brows, prompting the Angel to add, "I may be grounded, but that doesn't mean I can't perform a miracle where needed."

"Show off." Mason turned to Kira again. "Are you all right?"

She raised herself onto her hands and knees, back aching from the weight of its burden. Bruised was better than broken. She nodded.

The Angel strode lightly toward his new student and delivered his next set of instructions in a monotone.

"You'll get used to the weight, just as human infants become accustomed to walking on two feet. Soon, the act of taking flight will be automatic. Let the ground be your guide." He stopped in front of her, his shadow blending with the dark spill of her feathers. "Get up."

Kira set her jaw and obeyed. Her vessel rose while the tips of her wings brushed against the floor. She beat them again—this time while still suspended—and felt a rush of frigid air skate across her temple as she veered sharply toward the nearest wall. The impact left a shimmering halo around her field of vision as she corkscrewed to the floor inches from where Mason stood.

"I said don't help her!" the Angel boomed.

"I only take orders from Ansel," Mason countered, reaching for Kira's hand.

"In this room, you take orders from me. Now stand down—"

A fierce gale ripped through the dungeon. When Mason turned around, Kira was gone. The Angel advanced quickly, the cloudy blue pools of his eyes trained on his subordinate. They were allies, not equals, and he intended to prove this by any means necessary.

Sensing the Angel's rage, Mason backed toward the corner, orb raised like a shield. A Catcher's memories weren't caustic to an Angel the way they were to a malevolent, but a burst of light could still inflict damage on a creature accustomed to the dark.

The Angel matched Mason's defenses, summoning a melon-sized sphere from thin air. "Don't push me. My patience is extremely thin."

Mason extended his hand, letting the recollections drift between them.

"Stand down," the Angel repeated.

"We arrived together, and we will leave together—with or without you."

"I said *stand down*—"

Darkness descended on the room. Mason staggered back as shockwaves crashed over him. Kira straightened her legs, fanning her wings protectively.

"Get up," she told the Angel. "You've sat around here long enough. Now how do I find the others?"

"You're a malevolent," he reminded her. "Let your hunger lead you wherever it will."

"Two minutes ago you said the ground was my guide. Now I'm supposed to listen to my hunger?"

The Angel smiled humourlessly. "You said you had a connection with Samoia. That it called to you. Answer the call, and you'll find what you're looking for."

Kira closed her eyes. Just as clearly as she'd seen Dean spiraling into the blackness, she saw the tunnels and pathways take shape around her, each one invisible to her grounded comrades. With a powerful thrust of her wings, she took flight and disappeared through a portal near the ceiling, several hundred feet off the ground.

Love & War

Sarah lay alone in the dark, her pride wounded and her mind weak. The malevolent's likeness to Gabe had blasted through her defenses like a cannon ball. She'd come to Samoia to find her daughter and the crew, and now she was cut off from The Establishment—and with it, any chance of being rescued.

She activated her Keepsake again, casting Gabe's memory onto the wall. Once Ansel's most trusted advisor, he'd come to The Establishment a broken spirit: bitter, cynical, and determined to interfere in all of Sarah's attempts to execute Ansel's orders. Eventually, trapped in the human realm with another man's memories, he'd had no choice but to cooperate in her mission or risk an eternity in the in-between.

They'd conceived Kira while on the run from police. By the time Sarah had learned about their daughter's existence, Gabe had already regenerated, forcing her to juggle two seemingly impossible jobs: overseeing the smooth operation of the afterlife, and raising a creature that would never experience the unparalleled joy—and sorrow—of being human.

Sarah's ring flickered, causing the images to vanish. This had been the malevolent's plan all along: to use her past as an entry point for possession, to make her question herself so deeply that she wouldn't hesitate to hand over her power in exchange for total oblivion.

And really, what did it matter if she never returned to The Establishment? Ansel and the others would carry on as they had done before she'd arrived, and eventually someone else would take her place as his second-in-command. Kira might miss her for a while, but she still had Mason; the thought made Sarah unspeakably jealous. Samoia had taken Damien from her, and now she had no one to confide in. Everyone she'd ever loved was gone.

Sarah closed her eyes. When she opened them again, sensing a presence that hadn't been there before, she discovered a tumble of black hair, unyielding green eyes, and the bow-like curve of a falcon's wings hovering above her head.

Gabe?

But it couldn't be him. Could it? No, she was seeing things: another one of Samoia's illusions, no doubt. Gabe wasn't here, and yet the surge of relief was so intense that the glow from her Keepsake illuminated the entire cell—and with it, Kira's face.

"Mom?" She reached down to smooth the hair back from Sarah's brow as darkness enveloped them once more. "It's me."

"How did you get in? And what are…" Sarah nodded at the broad shadow that covered them like a blanket. "Those?"

Kira looked over her shoulder, shrugged, and said, "Wings. An Angel gave them to me."

"An Angel gave them to you," Sarah repeated slowly, processing each word. Kira nodded, unfazed by the puzzlement on her mother's face. "Where?"

"In the Devil's Throat. Mason and I were looking for the crew and we got lost and ended up in a room with a false ceiling. Then this… creature appeared and told us the story of how his kind went extinct, and that the only way out of the lair was to combine our abilities." Kira broke off, tracing the links in the chain snaking around Sarah's feet. "He also said to follow my hunger."

"And it led you here." Sarah reached for her daughter using her right hand only, in case Kira's instinct decided to take over. "Do you know the way out?"

"There's a series of pathways above and below this room. Some lead nowhere, and others go straight to the heart of Samoia. I heard voices down there. It might be the crew, or it might be nothing, but I think we should check." Kira's attention shifted to the shackles.

Following her daughter's gaze, Sarah explained, "It's a unique contraption—impossible to manipulate." She paused, gauging Kira's reaction. "You may need to go on without me."

Kira leaned in for a closer look. Upon further inspection, she noticed that the band was not solid metal, as its appearance had led her to believe, but a complex system of interlocking images. She turned the cuff slowly, trying to see the full picture without knowing the story behind it.

"It's a memory chain," she said, sitting back on her heels, "comprised of millions of repressed memories. Ansel showed me one of these once."

Sarah stared blankly. "Oh, did he? I find it odd that I wasn't consulted in this discussion."

"That's because you're not a malevolent." Kira went on, "It's not an easy thing to build, either: combing a subject's memories, determining which ones are the most painful, and extracting them from the Keepsake takes a tremendous amount of power—enough to destroy the chain's creator, in many cases."

"So, what you're saying is there's no hope of me getting out of here."

"I'm saying you're going to have to trust me."

Sarah eyed Kira's ring. Knowing that Ansel had been mentoring Kira in secret made her reluctant to trust either of them, but failure to return to The Establishment with the crew could jeopardize her position in the company. Who would the spirits rely on then?

She grasped Kira's hand. Almost immediately, a golden thread of light tied their Keepsakes together. The chamber transformed into a theatre, and the walls dissolved into a colourful panorama featuring grassy hills, ivory sand, and a turquoise belt around the wide waist of sky.

"This can't be right," Sarah argued, "it's too vivid."

"What is it?" Kira's eyes sparkled with wonder at the lacy white clouds overhead.

"It's a beach. I used to come here all the time when…" Sarah broke off and scanned the shoreline, hoping for a familiar face to pop up out of the frothing surf.

"But it is painful for you," Kira observed.

"This a cornerstone memory—the one I use in all my malevolent encounters. Painful or not, they can't break through a barrier this solid. Let's keep going."

Years passed in a matter of seconds. From the mundane to the marvelous, every moment in a human's life was documented—and it wasn't until they drew their dying breath that the minutiae of their existence came to light. Once entered into The Establishment's catalogue, and assigned a ring with a unique serial number, a spirit could access any detail from a previous life, good or bad, and use it to ward off evil—unless the evil found a use for it first.

Loosening her grip, Kira brought the train of recollections to a standstill. They were in a city now, surrounded by chunky grey buildings and the scent of scorched rubber. Smears of red and blue light glistened on the wet pavement. Pebbles of glass crunched under their feet. A pink pacifier, rendered redundant by the circumstances, lay on the ground a short distance away. Kira extended a hand toward it, only to freeze at the sound of Sarah's voice.

"Don't touch it. You'll spoil the memory."

It was incomplete: patches of darkness littered the scene like mourners at a funeral, and every time Sarah focused on them, the voids seemed to grow larger, absorbing more details from the incident. Half a car lay under a yellow traffic light, its windows replaced by gaping holes and writhing black smoke. At the centre of the crash site, a pool of nothingness spread toward the sidewalk. It wasn't often that she attended accidents like this one, but since there'd been a child involved, she'd had no choice. Ansel needed someone he could trust.

"Mom?" Kira gazed around at the rips in the sky where the walls of the chamber were visible. "What is this?"

"It's the memory I've been repressing—the night of Brody's death." Sarah briefly closed her eyes, centring herself amidst the chaos. When she opened them again, she saw the ghost of her brother, a once healthy thirty-eight-year-old gutted by grief and alcohol, standing before her.

"In my past life, I had an older brother named Brody," Sarah explained. More details started to trickle in, filling the empty spaces around them. "My death tore our family apart. Brody eventually lost his band, then his job, then his wife. All he had left at this point was his daughter, whom he named after me."

The vehicle Brody had been driving, a silver van with stickers on the rear inside window, faded into focus once more. Sarah took a step toward it, emptily assessing the damage.

"At thirty-six, he developed a drinking problem. I know this because I kept tabs on him over the years, even though it's against protocol to maintain a connection with the Living."

"Did Ansel know what you were doing?"

"I believe he did. That's why he sent me to collect Brody's soul." Sarah faced the body on the ground: a fleshy white airplane parked on a runway of blood. "As punishment."

The remaining shapes and colours snapped into view, completing the picture she had been trying to erase for years. Sarah looked down at the shackle on her foot. The shiny cuff turned to rust, crumbled, and blew away, taking the chain with it.

"I was so focused on the baby, I couldn't catch Brody," she said. "It's bad enough to see a ghost. It's even worse to create one."

She felt Kira's hand on her shoulder. The memory went up in smoke as Brody ran for the cover of an alleyway, doomed to haunt the intersection that had claimed him forever.

"What happened to the baby?" Kira asked.

"That's a story for another day," Sarah said as the ceiling strained under its own weight.

Kira crossed the room to the door. As she reached for the handle, a gust of warm air ruffled her hair and feathers. There was no hallway on the other side—only a vertical drop that ended in a pinprick of amber light.

"Is there a problem?" Sarah asked.

"Not for me," Kira replied, stepping aside. Sarah sidled up on her left and peered over the edge of the floor. Fist-sized stones rattled down the rough chimney and were quickly devoured by the blinding glow.

"Do you hear them?" Kira asked.

Sarah cocked her head, listening. "No," she said after a moment. "I don't hear anything."

Kira turned away from the shaft. Her eyes were the texture of black marble, with pink veins unspooling from the corners and forming jagged polygons as they intersected. Sarah retreated, tucking her left hand behind her back.

"Nothing?" Kira said, sounding disappointed. "Are you sure?"

"I'm sure." Sarah relaxed her hold on the orb. She'd had to defend herself against Gabe once, but it was clear he'd known what he was doing—unlike Kira, whose face was mired in fear as well as hunger.

Kira stared down at her hands, where hundreds of short, sharp quills were poking through the surface of her skin. "It's just me then."

"Do you think you can get to them?"

"I—I think—" Kira doubled over as a mass of smoke from her smoldering essence choked her mid-sentence. When it passed, it left her feeling like she could swallow the sun whole—and still be starving.

The dark Angel extended to her full height again, and Sarah straightened her back, adopting the stony countenance of a gargoyle.

"Kira," she began. "Don't listen to the voices. Listen to *me*. You can control this." The orb solidified in her grasp as a myriad of images swirled inside the crystalline bomb.

Kira spread her wings, casting a mammoth shadow on the ceiling. She bore down on Sarah like a hawk, a look of calculation clouding the stormy red eyes.

"Kira, honey, listen to me. You *can* control this."

"I can't. It's who I am."

"We're defined by the choices we make, and you can choose to rise above your impulses. That's why the Angel gave you wings." Sarah lowered her guard. "Use them, Kira."

With a vicious flap, Kira lifted off the ground. As she stroked toward her target, a cement fragment, pried loose from its rocky cleft by the thunderous currents of air, descended alongside her. The chunk of debris struck Sarah behind her left ear. She folded forward, clenching her fists in pain.

The orb disintegrated with a bang. Kira ducked, but couldn't avoid the shockwave that caught her wings and propelled her backwards. She crashed against the doorframe, then tumbled over the edge to the sound of Sarah screaming her name.

Kira fell, and kept falling until her sense of time became distorted. Her wings refused to cooperate. Her remaining four limbs struck out as if faced with an invisible attacker, and after several failed attempts to deploy her feathery parachute, Kira was able to gain the upper hand over gravity.

Sarah was still screaming her name by the time she dizzily fastened herself to a handhold.

"Kira! Are you alright?"

Kira adjusted her grip on the gnarled protuberance. The shock of the fall had left her wing feathers disheveled and her mind sputtering with possibilities. She fluffed the kinks out of her fifth and sixth limbs, then craned her head back to deliver an update.

"I'm fine! But that's the last time I'm taking advice from you."

Sarah drifted back from the opening and appraised the demolition-in-progress with grim appreciation: not only could Samoia move mountains and flood fields as easily as Sarah could extract a soul from a dying person's body, but it did it all with a smile. A wide crack split the ceiling like a grin on an old man's face, revealing a hint of the playful child within. She would need to find another way out, and soon, if she didn't want to be stuck babysitting a young planet.

Near the base of the shaft, Kira had almost collected her wits enough to devise a plan for finding the crew. The light she'd seen from above came from a wide conduit that reeked of stale water and had more boils than a witch's nose. The voices were louder now, magnified by the interplay of proximity and architecture.

She lowered herself to the ground and shook the excess moisture off her back. It felt as if the elements had gone to war with each other: water had invaded the air and the fire fueling her soul could easily be snuffed by the army of stones above. Kira advanced silently toward enemy lines and soon came to a room with a high ceiling, pale walls, and a cocky orator who laughed at his own jokes. The colour of his eyes told her the rest.

"So then he says, 'The day you become God is the day pigs fly', and I say, 'Then I suppose that day is today, because look what blew in from the mountains!'" The alpha snarled at the Angel, half-hidden behind his built-in partition. "Isn't that right, Bjorn?"

Bjorn didn't answer, and Kira couldn't blame him. She'd been the butt of enough hurtful jokes to understand why it was called the punchline.

The malevolent continued. "Now, if I recall correctly, it was *your* idea to take a shortcut to the training grounds, was it not?" He waited. His eyes were the colour of days-old blood: crimson bordering on onyx, with the faintest trace of copper wreathing the edges. When no answer came, his delight increased tenfold. "I'll take that as a yes."

She stepped forward. The malevolent's expression brightened at the sight of the long, black hair and even more impressive wingspan, and his mouth watered reflexively at the unfettered glow pulsing through her thin, white shirt. On this planet, he was king—and tonight he would prove it by feasting like one.

"Whatever happened to the others is not his fault," she began, casting a glance in Bjorn's direction. "If it hadn't been for him, I would've never gotten my wings. There's good in everything… and everyone."

"I couldn't agree more." Flicking his eyes toward the huddle of red-clad hostages, the malevolent turned back to Kira and said, "Let's prove it, shall we?"

"We?"

"You are a malevolent, aren't you?"

"Part," Kira corrected, catching Mason's eyes, "and even then…"

The malevolent reached for her left hand and yanked her into the centre of his personal stage. His gaze sank to her Keepsake, where a pattern of red, silver, and gold coiled inward like a snake.

"Nice ring," he hissed. "Let's see if it works."

Turning toward the Angel, Kira's captor applied her hand to the misshapen wing. He cried out in pain as a bolt of electricity linked predator to prey. Her fingertips became numb, and soon the feeling spread to the rest of her limbs, culminating in a soothing warmth that made her drowsy with pleasure.

When the malevolent broke the connection at last, a black handprint remained on the soft white fan. Kira's eyes opened slowly, revealing a similar, sooty hue.

"Did you feel that?" he asked. She nodded, unable to take her eyes off her subject. Satisfaction carved deep lines around the corners of her mouth as she grinned, watching the Angel's normally impervious field disintegrate into a mesh of insecurities. So many doubts, so many possibilities.

The puppet master explained, "It's like an all-you-can-eat buffet. Angels are a source of infinite energy, you know. Unfortunately, they're virtually impossible to catch." He steered her focus elsewhere. Kira's hunger had transformed the room into a dark, undefined space. Her comrades were no longer individuals she knew and recognized, but vague pulses of light joined in a constellation for which she had no name. To them, she must've looked like a black hole intent on consuming everything in its path.

Mason shifted; his concern over Kira's wellbeing made him appear brighter than his companions, and her knees trembled with a troubling desire to possess him.

In the malevolent's steaming grip, Kira's hand froze. A wall had gone up inside her the moment she tasted Mason's fear, cold as a spring stream.

"Take it," the fiend ordered, holding Kira's hand above Mason's chest. A sapphire marble hovered tantalizingly close to her fingertips, begging to be plucked from the tangle of veins around it.

"That's it." The dead weight clinging to Kira's arm came to life with a shudder. "I'd do it myself, but I'd rather watch you suffer."

Kira pressed harder, her hand held flat against Mason's form like a door she'd resisted opening until now. His essence unraveled and writhed like stretched yarn as the power shifted between them.

The light in his eyes vanished. With the last of his energy depleted, his head fell forward and his field faded like smoke, leaving a bitter taste in Kira's mouth.

A hand brushed her crown in slow, patronizing strokes. Waves of grief lapped against Kira's eyes, but she held on tight to her tears.

"Take your hands off my daughter," came a sharp voice from the doorway.

The malevolent leered at Ansel's deputy with a fluorescent grin.

"Sarah," he rasped, running his eyes down her tattered uniform. "How kind of you to join us."

"I'd be wary of my kindness if I were you. I hear it can be lethal."

"What can I say? I'm a glutton for punishment."

Sarah smiled. A satiny blue aura engulfed her left hand as she skimmed a fresh batch of memories off the surface of her stone.

"I almost forgot to thank you for the memories," she said as the orb solidified in her grasp. "Seems like I've caught Brody after all."

She discharged her weapon. Kira's keeper recoiled from the blast, severing the connection with a sizzling crack. The current flowed back into Kira's arm and through her hand before spooling in Mason's chest like a roll of film. When he opened his eyes, his face was the picture of health, bright as a television in pitch-black living room.

Across the room, the malevolent shook his head and stood up slowly. He directed his vitriol at Sarah as his posse emerged from the shadows.

"You shouldn't have come here," he snarled.

"What can I say? I'm a glutton for punishment."

The malevolent threw his head back and laughed, the sound echoing off the bone-white walls.

"Then let us feast! Last one standing gets the flock."

Sarah narrowed her eyes in consideration. She wondered if "the flock" included the members of his army, which could power The Establishment indefinitely and eliminate the need for dangerous missions in the future.

"I'm waiting," he taunted, his voice rising half an octave as he stared at her. "Unless, of course, you'd rather admit defeat now."

"No."

"No? Not even if it means sparing your daughter's life?" He motioned to her protégé, standing a short distance away from her peers.

"What are you talking about?"

"I'm talking about a trade: their presence for hers." He motioned to the group of spirits huddled in the corner. "Let's face it, Sarah: what you really want is a family. I can't say I blame you. I mean, think of all the people you lost... all the faces you'll never see again. Your mother. Father. Brody. Damien." He smirked. "Gabe."

"Keep his name out of your mouth," Sarah said coolly.

"All I'm saying is... Kira is all you have left. The only thing standing between you and that cold, dark place. You lose her, you lose everything."

"Mom, no!" Kira chimed in. "He's just trying to get inside your head."

"Smart girl," the malevolent purred. "Great minds think alike, don't they?"

"She's nothing like you."

"Are you absolutely certain about that?"

The grating of a monstrous, unseen machine heralded another change in the landscape. A neon pall spiraled overhead, blurring the edges of the room as well as the faces gathered in the corners.

"Last chance," their leader said with a smirk, holding Sarah's icy gaze. "And if you can't make a choice, Samoia will make it for you."

As he said this, a thunderous crack split the floor. Kira released Mason's hand and spread her wings, shielding the crew from the gust of scorching air that fountained out of the chasm. Sarah scrambled back from the edge and looked over at her daughter, whose wide green eyes were fixed on the pulsating light buried at the bottom.

"Kira, look at me," Sarah said firmly, relieved when she obeyed. "Take Bjorn and the crew and get out of here."

"But what about you?"

"Please don't argue with me. I may be your mother, but I'm also your boss." A wedge of rock plummeted toward the mechanical heart as Sarah adjusted her footing, keeping her gaze steady on the malevolent's face. "Do what I say—and trust me."

"I'm not leaving."

"I don't want to lose you, and Ansel can't afford these many casualties." Sarah indicated the crew. "I'll be fine—and if not, you're more than capable of replacing me."

Kira stood frozen; whether it was in fear or insubordination Sarah couldn't say for sure. All she knew was that she'd been right about one thing: everything went on—people, planets, even the afterlife.

She stared down the chimney at her fate, then up at her nemesis in cool resignation.

"Have you made your choice?" he asked.

Sarah nodded.

The malevolent shifted into a column of smoke. He hovered above the divide as a spinning black mass, drawing heat, light, and even solid particles of rock into his orbit. The ground under Sarah's feet became loose and she retreated again, pressing her back flat against the wall.

Then the screams started. One by one, the remaining malevolents rose to join their messiah. They circled him tirelessly, forming a dense shell around the luminescent core. Even as Sarah began rallying her defenses, she knew it was futile to fight back. Kira would be okay. It was the only promise Ansel had ever made.

Darkness blanketed the room. Out of the corner of her eye, Sarah saw Mason escorting the crew through a narrow crevice in the wall. Bjorn, who was considerably taller than the average Catcher, sized up the cleft in disgust, then angled himself to fit the path.

Kira was the only one who didn't move. The only one for whom freedom came at a cost.

Sarah nodded, struggling to keep her emotions contained.

"It's okay," she said above the gale. "Just go." This memory, like all the others, was already carved in stone. It may have been enough to deter an individual malevolent, or even a small, leaderless pack, but the threat Sarah faced now would only grow if it knew the depth of her fear, or the size of the hole Kira was leaving behind. A mother's love was both her best weapon and her greatest weakness.

The malevolent screeched, then burst through the wall of ash and smoke toward his target.

A rush of air plastered Sarah against the crumbling wall as a black object shot into the malevolent's path. A dizzying display of amber and ivory meshed and swirled like the optical cages on a Monarch butterfly's wings, trapping the eye with its beauty. The creatures locked together like two links in a chain before tumbling into the fiery grave thousands of feet below. A trail of half-burned feathers lingered in their wake.

Down they fell, gaining speed as they corkscrewed past the layers of rock and root. Kira could feel her wings disintegrating as the heat from the blazing core intensified. The malevolent's hand fastened itself to her wrist. A pair of ruby spheres emerged from the elongated face, then the mouth opened and swallowed the last of her pride.

Her feathers flaked away in sooty reams. A dozen feet more, and the malevolent released her arm, flinging Kira into the craggy wall. The darkness embraced her like an old friend.

"Kira!" Sarah leaned over the edge of her perch. The smoke and the feathers were gone and the light continued to flicker, confirming her worst fears. "Kira!"

No answer came from the deep. Mason, across from her, was equally silent.

Suddenly, a flash of white lit the darkness. Bjorn lifted into the air with a cumbersome flap and a stifled grunt of pain, then dove off the lip and into the jaws of the beast.

His shoulder burned. The splintered bones crackled as they rubbed together, but still he descended, wings beating frantically against his back. The flailing outline of a falling star brought his senses into focus. Kira was little more than a speck of black paint on an orange canvas, but as long as he could see her, there was a chance she could be saved—just like she'd saved him.

The shaft narrowed, forcing Bjorn to tuck his wings behind his back. His vertical form punctured the thick layer of warmth surrounding Samoia's core, and like any animal unlucky enough to be the recipient of a hunter's arrow, the planet seized in shock before collapsing around them.

Kira was no longer flailing, but falling gently into the arms of oblivion. Bjorn reached for her and missed. The rocks kept coming. One of the missiles nicked the tip of his wing and he jerked sideways, stretching the distance between himself and his target. He dropped again, ignoring the flames racing over his skin and clothes. He made another grab for Kira's hand, and this time they connected.

Bjorn fanned his wings, slowing their descent. The strands of minerals and other impurities skidded into focus as he reeled Kira's limp form into his arms and winged back toward the opening, fighting gravity with each powerful thrust.

Ten feet from the top, the Angel reached for Mason's hand.

"Pull me up—quickly," Bjorn ordered. Mason complied without question this time, dragging the seven-foot savior and his unconscious burden out of the darkness. Sarah lay prone on the cliff beside Mason, grasping for the edges of her daughter's clothes until she was safe in her arms again.

The chasm sealed itself. Black and white wing fragments littered the floor; the larger quills lay smoldering in the dark, gilded in Samoia's fury.

Sarah swept the hair out of Kira's face and massaged her cheeks.

"Kira?" Sarah rocked back and forth, fighting down the panic in her voice as her child swayed lifelessly in her arms. "Come on, honey, wake up. It's over now."

Mason stood up and turned toward Bjorn. The ancient spirit knelt on the floor. His smoky plumage cascaded down his back like a wizard's robe sequined with embers and beads of silver blood.

Mason gazed down at his hands, pulsing with the remnants of the orb he'd prepared to confront Kira's captor. But what could he have done? By the time he'd returned from escorting the crew to safety, Kira had already chosen her fate. He spread his fingers, turned his palms outward to release the surplus of energy, and let his arms rest at his sides.

Bjorn staggered to his feet and turned to look at Sarah, lost in the motions of her grief.

"Kira, please," Sarah persisted. Mason stood over her, his expression strained. "Come on, baby, open your eyes. Please."

Sarah removed her hand from Kira's face and placed it on her chest. Tangled in the web of shadows lining her cavity, the smooth bulb of Kira's essence dimmed to an autumnal brown, heralding the cold, dark days to come.

Sarah shook her head, growing increasingly desperate. "Kira, please. Please look at me. I'm sorry I let you come here. I'm sorry."

The remaining colour drained from the young Catcher's face. Even her Keepsake turned white. Her eyelids, fringed with thick black lashes like her father's, flickered reflexively before adopting the breathtaking stillness of a frozen lake.

Bjorn lifted Kira's hand and examined the blanched Keepsake. He thumbed the stone, coaxing her most vivid memories to the surface.

Mason came forward as well, his ring beaming optimistically in the darkness of the lair.

"Here," he said, hovering over the trio. "I don't know how much energy I have left, but she needs it more than I do."

Bjorn raised his hand. "Save it. You'll have your chance to help her once we're en route to The Establishment."

"But——"

"Stand down." The Angel spoke calmly this time, his attention riveted on his task.

Mason came close to protesting, but bit his tongue and retreated to the corner to sulk. There, he rested his elbows on his knees and watched Ansel's best airman trace Kira's form, from her elegant fingers to the rigid soles of her boots. He squirmed at the sight of Bjorn's lingering touch, not out of jealousy but out of fear. What if this didn't work? He still had so much to teach her, and so much to learn. Mason couldn't imagine a life without Kira, much less an afterlife where she didn't exist.

"Do you know what my job was at The Establishment?" Bjorn asked as he continued to stroke Kira's arm. His fingers skimmed the surface of her field, causing the invisible particles encasing her vessel to vibrate.

Sarah shook her head, transfixed by the ritualistic movements.

The Angel smiled. "Neither do I. It's been so long." He passed his hand over the horizontal figure again. Bit by bit, the colour returned to her lips, eyelids, and fingernails. Beneath her uniform and through the skin of her torso, a faint blush of light illuminated her essence, sparking fresh hope in her mother's eyes.

"Have you ever restored a spirit, Sarah?"

"Yes. My niece's." She met Bjorn's inquiring gaze. She couldn't begin to guess the being's age, but his eyes contained galaxies that hadn't been documented in any of Ansel's history books.

Sarah explained, "Ansel sent me to collect her spirit. My brother was... troubled by my death. I could see it in his eyes, that emptiness that had been there for years. After he ran away, and I returned to The Establishment with his daughter's soul, Ansel said that the only way to keep Brody from disappearing entirely was to give the baby back her memories of him, even if she didn't remember anything from the crash.

"We left the incubator and went up to the reversal chamber. Ansel laid her out on the table and told me I only had a couple of minutes to rewrite history. She was so small, this doughy little person in the middle of a cold, white room. She smiled at me, with that small pink mouth and those big blue eyes, and all I could think about was Kira. If I lost her, I'd hope like hell that whoever took her would bring her back..."

Sarah paused, looking down at the spoons of Kira's eye sockets and the knifelike edge of her nose. Bjorn's touch had thawed out her legs and fingertips, but they still had miles to go before they saw the verdant splendor of her eyes. At the back of her mind, Sarah questioned whether they'd ever reach their destination.

"I approached my niece's spirit on that table and I looked into her eyes and said, 'You won't remember any of this.' Sometimes the older ones do, but no one ever believes them when they try and explain what they saw." She shook her head and adjusted Kira's weight, or what little of it remained. "I took a broken soul and I put it back together: every memory, every tickle, twinge, and tear she'd ever felt or would feel. Every smile. Every laugh. Every lullaby Brody had ever sung. When it was done, Ansel picked her up and carried her out of the room.

"She's nine now and does karate. Whenever she tells people about her aunt Sarah, they chalk it up to imagination." Sarah smiled, a faraway look clouding her eyes. "He'd be so proud of her."

The Angel's lips curved upwards. He laid Kira's hand in the middle of her abdomen, and within moments, her Keepsake's glow filled the room. As the shadows cleared from her face, her brows furrowed at the invasion of light. She jerked her head sideways, and when she opened her eyes at last, the first thing she saw was the sky-blue hue of freedom.

Mason leapt to his feet as Sarah helped her daughter to sit up. Kira's arms quivered like a newborn lamb's first steps, black spots stained her vision, and her essence strobed against her papery flesh. But she was here. She was here, and all she wanted now was to go home.

Mason started toward the pair, only to be stopped by a strong hand on his shoulder.

"You'll have your chance," the Angel assured him.

"How did you do it?"

Bjorn lifted his right shoulder, and the corresponding wing rose with it. "Like I said: Miracles are my specialty."

He stepped forward. Ironically, without her wings, Kira felt light as a feather. Two vermillion welts were all that remained of the sleek black attachments; her shoulder blades felt like hot coals as Bjorn lifted her into his arms.

As if reading his mind, Mason bent down and picked up one of the quills.

"Every memorable trip needs a souvenir," he said.

"So it does." Sarah faced the Angel and his precious cargo. "We should find the crew. Ansel will be expecting us back soon."

"Most of us," Mason corrected, glimpsing the receding outline of the recently freed prisoner.

"Nice work out there, soldier." Sarah followed Bjorn and Kira toward the only exit, beyond which she heard the dull chatter of their weary comrades. "But next time, try following orders."

Royal Welcome

"In spite of everything that happened, I can't deny that this mission was a success. You located the crew, you freed Bjorn, and most importantly, you saved Kira." Ansel's gaze locked onto Sarah, sitting across from him in the stark white boardroom. "I'm sorry for your loss. Damien will be deeply missed."

"I know." She continued to stare at the surface of the table, watching a star trapped in its obsidian depths scatter like dandelion seeds. Stars didn't mourn the loss of their own, but she was already feeling destitute and extended a morsel of sympathy to the supernova's cosmic counterparts.

After a moment of silence, she raised her eyes to the stony overseer and said, "I didn't do any of the things you listed. The credit should go to Kira and Mason."

"And it will. I'm putting both of them on a leave of absence to rest."

"And Bjorn? I don't even know what Angels do here."

A smile creased the granite mouth. Whoever Bjorn was or used to be, his standing at The Establishment had not been tarnished by his million-year hiatus. And it wasn't hard to see why: compared to the average Catcher, he was a giant. From the second Ansel had joined his dumbstruck subordinates in the hangar, it was clear that life—and death—would never be the same.

"You told me Angels didn't exist," Sarah persisted.

"Up until Bjorn returned, that was true. Over the millennia, I attempted to make contact with the team stranded on Samoia but was unsuccessful. Eventually, I had no choice but to assume the worst."

"And no attempt was made to rescue them?"

"I didn't have the technology. I had only assumed control of The Establishment a couple centuries earlier and was more concerned with keeping the gears of existence turning. But now…" He tracked the path of a comet, its tail sizzling like a sparkler as it veered into the darkness of the universe. "Things are different. And much of it is thanks to you."

"If you're asking me to go on another rescue mission, my answer is no. My daughter almost succumbed out there. She needs me to stay and take care of her."

"She does. That's why I'm calling on someone else."

"Why not Jonathon? He needs to leave that basement sometime, and the trip will be good for his research into the migratory patterns of malevolents."

Ansel chuckled. "With his propensity for destabilization sickness, I wouldn't even be able to get him in the hangar." He rose slowly, shouldering the weight of his decision. "No, I don't think I'll send Jonathon."

"Who else has that much experience in dealing with malevolents? Besides Damien…"

"An old friend of yours. I believe you'll remember him well."

Ansel extended his hand toward the doors. The twin sheets of frosted glass glided open at his encouragement, and a figure with thick, peppery hair entered the room.

Sarah stood up, her mouth dropping open in shock.

"You rang?" Gabe said, looking at Ansel. Pointing a finger at his ear, he added, "And seriously: tinnitus? That's how we're communicating now?"

"I didn't want to scare the children by showing up unannounced." Ansel gestured to the woman across the desk. "You'll remember Sarah."

She approached their visitor slowly. Unlike the rest of Ansel's staff, Gabe's contract with The Establishment was indefinite. He'd served several years as the Grim Reaper before being demoted to Spirit Catcher, while still retaining his skills and the power to act on Ansel's behalf. He'd killed with merely a glance, and Sarah believed that if she had a heart, it would've stood still in her chest at the sight of him now.

She wrapped her arms around him. After a brief pause, his field meshed with hers, sending a familiar tingle through the core of her being.

Ansel stepped out from behind the desk and approached the door with his hands folded behind his back.

"I'll give you both some time to get reacquainted," he said.

Gabe released her. He'd aged considerably since their last encounter, but his jade green eyes still smoldered with mischief and his hair bristled defiantly, ensnaring any comb that had the audacity to cross it. Without thinking, Sarah reached up to tame the silver porcupine.

Gabe grinned. "We meet again, Miss Galloway."

"So we do." Sarah removed her fingers, looking him over in a blend of curiosity and disbelief. "How long has it been?"

"Forty-seven years, nine months, two weeks, one day, thirteen hours, fifty-two minutes, and six seconds."

"Really?"

"Well, the forty-seven years part is true. I made the rest up."

"I don't understand. You regenerated. How are you here?"

"I'm here in spirit, Sarah. My body is currently watching The Skunk Monk for the one hundredth time with my twins."

"You have twins?" she replied, arching her brows.

"And a teenage daughter, named Sophie. Believe me: running errands in the afterlife is about as exciting as it gets for me."

"Good to see you haven't changed. Not on the inside anyway." Sarah shook her head. "Now, I'm assuming Ansel has already briefed you on the mission."

"The mission. Right. And is there any particular reason why he's sending me and not his precious chosen one?"

"I have to stay here… to look after our daughter."

Gabe's eyes widened, and all traces of mockery vanished from his face.

She led the way to the doors. "Come with me."

When they entered the room, they found Kira lying on a raised platform. A thin, white gown covered her horizontal form to her knees, making the reams of jet-black hair appear darker than the edge of the universe. Seated on a chair at her bedside was Bjorn, his left arm folded in a sling that encompassed the collapsed bulk of his broken wing. His expression cleared at the sight of Kira's visitors. He stood up cautiously, looking between Sarah and the man who accompanied her.

"Bjorn," Sarah said, acknowledging the wounded guardian before turning to Gabe. "I'd like you to meet Gabe Conway—Kira's father. Gabe, this is Bjorn, one of Ansel's Elite."

"Mr. Conway," Bjorn stated, a smile crossing his dark brown face. "Infamous or not, it's an honour to finally meet you."

"My reputation precedes me—by a spectacular margin of time, it would seem."

"Word travels fast between universes. Spend a million years in the Devil's Throat and you're bound to hear some stories."

"How is she?" Sarah asked, shifting the conversation back to Kira.

Bjorn explained, "Stable, although she awoke recently mumbling something I couldn't decipher. It might be worth checking her Keepsake to see what she remembers." With another glance at the unconscious spirit, Bjorn adjusted his immobile arm and said, "I'll give you two some privacy. I'm sure you have a lot to catch up on."

In the Angel's absence, the room felt vast. A column of light descended from the ceiling, illuminating the table and tower of drawers set into the wall behind it. Sometimes, repairing a broken spirit was as simple as reconnecting the mind to the essence; other times, it was a complicated process involving memory removal, field recalibration, and, in extreme cases, purging parasitic energy from the affected host. Since returning from Samoia, Kira had undergone a battery of tests and procedures and now lay in a state of temporary oblivion to avoid damaging her luminous core. Sarah shone a light on Kira's abdomen, encouraged by the rosy haze piercing the gown.

"Good to know we can still clear a room," Gabe joked, moving to Kira's other side. "I'll have to remember to call you the next time my in-laws overstay their welcome."

"Do you still live in the big house on Jacobson?"

He shrugged, his face sagging under the weight of time. "Define 'living.'" He circled the platform, seeing Kira from every angle before turning to Sarah with a haunted expression. "You don't even know how lucky you are, do you?"

"Define 'lucky,'" she returned, crossing her arms as she leaned against one of the drawers. "Some time ago, Ansel sent me to collect the spirit of my deceased niece. My brother had been at the wheel at the time of her death and also succumbed to his injuries. He ran away from me and was never seen again. Sooner or later, everyone I've ever known or loved will cross my path and I won't even be able to share a coffee with them or hear about their day. So, you tell me, Gabe, just how *lucky* I am to spend an eternity without a human connection. Without a life."

His face relaxed, smoothing away the rough folds of skin trapped between his brows. The body he'd inhabited previously had been lean, toned, and sharp around the edges like broken glass, making every attempt at affection a potentially lethal endeavour. Now, at forty-seven Earth years, he'd settled into a form that made up for the lost intimacy, with pillows of skin around his neck and jaw and the weight of long nights stacked on his hips and shoulders. Failing health aside, his juniper green eyes remained untamed, and in their infinite depths Sarah caught a glimpse of the Samoian wilderness, filled with monsters that never slept.

"That day everything went south at The Establishment," Sarah began, reading the incremental shifts in his energy as he hunched over Kira's form, "you said 'once a reaper, always a reaper.' Do you remember that conversation?"

"I distinctly recall you stabbing me in the leg. I may have given you the abridged version of my job description, too, but it's been so long I don't see why it matters."

"Okay, one: you stabbed me. *I* saved your life. Two, it matters because your daughter—our daughter—had an unfortunate encounter with an alpha malevolent who has since gone underground—literally. He's taken possession of an entire planet, and if he gets close enough to Earth, he may jump ship to look for a new host, or distribute his energy across many hosts." Sarah straightened and walked over to where Gabe stood. "The only creature that can catch a spirit that powerful is a reaper, and you're as experienced as they come. A supreme being, capable of infinite destruction."

His right eyebrow lifted coolly, emphasizing the smirk that twisted on his lips. "I never thought I'd hear you flatter me again, Miss Galloway."

"I never thought I'd have to grovel for your cooperation again either."

"A match made in a poorly run paradise." He sobered, and with a small gesture at Kira, asked, "So, where is this rogue planet, and how do I get there?"

"We're not entirely sure, but as soon as we locate it, you'll be the first one on a Commander."

"You know, it's a shame you won't be in attendance. Like Pegasus Boy said, we have a lot to catch up on."

"I won't be there in spirit, but you'll be outfitted with an earpiece that connects directly to space traffic control, where I will be supervising the mission. Once you quarantine the alpha and disband the pack, Ansel will decide whether to destroy the planet or… rehabilitate it, make it fit for human habitation."

"Well, it can't be any worse than the cesspool I just came from." Unfastening his hands from the cool metal slab, he traced the ivory plateau of Kira's forehead with his finger, committing her shape to memory. "And when I come back, you can introduce us properly."

"It's a date." Sarah nodded at the door. "Head up to the wardrobe and we'll get you out of those human clothes and into something more appropriate."

Gabe bowed, his smile lingering as he departed. "As you wish, your highness."

JESSICA INGOLD is the author of numerous books for young adult readers as well as countless blogs and newspaper articles. With over ten years of experience in writing and self-publishing, her goal is to craft stories that resonate with book enthusiasts of all ages.

www.ingramcontent.com/pod-product-compliance
Lightning Source LLC
Chambersburg PA
CBHW060626130626
46555CB00002B/683